This book is dedicated to
Judi H.
Leslie.
Criss C.
Lydia F.
For all that you do to not only encourage but actively help me
in pursuing my dreams not only as a writer but as a trainer.
You are my pillars and I am blessed beyond measure to call you
my friends, my family.

Chapter 1: Home

Horses in kill pens come from all walks of life. Ranch horses, show horses, broodmares, etc. Every breed and color imaginable can be found in the kill pens, awaiting their death. Everything from newborns to the aged, sound and lame, death does not discriminate. Often when looking for a companion or equine partner, rescue horses, auctions and kill pens are home to the overlooked prospects of perfection that we crave in our lives.
Sitting, awaiting death, may be the horse of your dreams.

Each horse there has a story, a past, a life that they have lived. Often, we simply don't want to read the present and therefore discount their past and rob them of a future.

May 1

There are no days off when you work on a ranch, there is always something that needs to be done. I spend my days helping my people tend fences, move cattle, brand calves among other duties assigned to me. I have had three foals, all the most beautiful children. My daughter often works with me in the fields, carrying her person, our neighbor. We work in heat, rain, snow and anything that the day might bring.

The old man who lives next door once owned my mother many years ago, and now his partner is my daughter. She tells me often of his kindness and his patience, and we exchange stories when it's time to camp down for the evening. Our people are very different, hers and mine. My owner brought me home as a young horse, along with Duke, my cousin. My person is a gruff old man and I wonder if it is because he is stiff in his joints, as I am now. We battle often, and the fighting is sometimes very fierce, he is a warrior who does not tolerate mistakes from his animal partners. Though as I say that we battle, that is not entirely correct. He battles and I often receive the brunt of that anger. Everything from a small miscalculation to not lining him up right to rope a calf. We are expected to carry not only our own burdens, but also take responsibility for the mistakes of our partners. I have been his partner for 20 years, and there is not much fight left in me, only flee. This is the story of my last few days at home, in my fields, and with my herds.
My name is Lady, and I am a 22 year old bay ranch mare.

May 2

We went out to brand calves. I am just about the best horse in a branding pen. I will line them up and hold them all day long if I have to. I have a stifle that is starting to act up a little bit, but I am still strong and do my job well. Duke and I joked while we worked, moving calves and holding them for branding. Sally was in charge of pushing the calves into the pen for us. She is an all business kind of horse. I really like her as a working partner, but she has no sense of humor. Never has. There is only one ranch hand that can really get her to work well, and that's because he is a bigger prick than she is, but they work together like a machine.

Duke is built like I am, except that he is a grey. He's 14.3, stout but as agile as a barn cat, smart and sarcastic too. He's a good ol boy. We work and tease and give each other hell. He is sure footed and quick witted and we have been partners in this work for many years. The person he carries, he has been carrying for 14 of his years here. They both have the same personality, goofy but damn talented.

Sally is on the smaller side, she is from "cutting stock", and she is a royal pain in the ass. She doesn't like people and I don't really think she even likes horses. She is a deep liver chestnut and can work a cow with the best of them, but she is lacking in personality. Her ranch hand likes her, because he doesn't have any personality either, he's a short stocky guy with a gruff demeanor. The other ranch hands will tease him from time to time, but he never teases back. Just sits on his little horse and huffs. I think I only ever heard him tell a joke once and everyone was so surprised that the little tough guy blushed and never joked again. But I have to give them credit, boy can they work.

May 3

We got turned out to graze for the evening, after a long day of checking fences and doctoring cattle. Sometimes it feels like these long days are wearing on me, but they are all I have ever known, and I am good at what I do. My stifle is a little stiff, but as the days warm up, it gets easier, those snow days and cold nights were a little rougher on me this year, it took me just a little longer to loosen up before I was moving smooth. Even so, I was able to mask the discomfort, as is the nature of our kind.

Two of the mares that work here are in another pasture, one of them has already foaled, a cute little roan colt, the other mare is due any day and looks as uncomfortable as they come. In a couple of years those babies will probably be out here working too. They don't tend to keep a lot of horses here, but there are a handful of us on rotation, on the long days one ranch hand may ride anywhere from one to four horses depending on the work we are doing that day. My owner is the only one who never switches out, I am his horse and that is the beginning and the end of it. Sometimes I think he just likes to show off that his horse can go all day and the others can't, other times I think it's his way of putting me to the test.

Duke has been feeling good all evening, exaggerating his prowess in catching and doctoring cows. They were familiar and wildly overplayed stories of our typical work. I liked listening to him though, he always made the work fun. The days go faster with a partner like Duke. We are about the same age, I think Duke is a year older than me. God when did we get old? Well other than that one stifle, I certainly don't feel old and you would never guess that Duke is 23, he acts like he's 6.

May 5

Something was wrong with the hay they fed us this evening, it smelled funny to me. Duke said that it tasted fine and proceeded to eat his and mine. After a couple of hours, Duke started to get sick to his stomach. He started biting at his sides and kicking at his belly. "Damn, Lady I think you were right not to eat, I'm not feeling so hot. Maybe I'll lay down for a bit." I looked over to the other side of the pasture to see that Sally was down also. She is usually off by herself so I hadn't noticed earlier. I don't know how long she had been down, but she was already thrashing and her belly looked BIG.

I kicked Duke, "Get up!" Duke moaned and started to roll, I went and checked on Sally, she was in a bad way. She was bloated badly and had been thrashing, she was already pretty tore up.

"Lady?! What the hell is going on?!" Her eyes were huge, she was in an extreme amount of pain and she was terrified. I had never even seen this mare nervous. Yet here she was genuinely panicked. Where the hell is the night ranch hand?

I headed back to Duke and he was thrashing hard and groaning. I called out and heard my own voice echo into the night. I know he is out here somewhere, he checks the mares that are pregnant about every hour or so. I called again. I heard one noise start as another one stopped. It was a confusing mixture and I had to separate each noise.

The footsteps of the ranch hand, coming quick, that's what I was hearing. But Sally had stopped thrashing. When the ranch hand got to the pasture he saw Duke down. "Oh shit! Lady, where's Sally?"I looked over into the night and her lifeless frame was oddly shaped in the moonlight. "Damn." He got on his phone to my owner. 'Duke is down and in a bad way. Lady is up. I think Sally is already dead." There was panic in his voice. They talked for about 2 minutes, the ranch hand pulled the phone away from his ear and grimaced; I heard my owner yelling over the phone, "There is no time for a vet, if he's that bad dammit!"

My owner was there in about another minute, blasting down the drive in his truck. He got to the pasture where I was standing by a now violently thrashing Duke. My owner walked up looked at Duke and sighed. He timed, aimed and shot Duke in the head. While it was a hard shock to me, it was a kindness shown to Duke, in order to end his suffering. They moved me to a stall in the barn and discussed burying the two dead horses in the morning, which was only a few hours away.

May 7

I worked with some of the other horses today. It was solemn and everyone was quiet, on one hand we were happy to be alive, on the other hand ignoring the fact that we had lost two of our best horses. We checked fences and moved cattle, turned cows out with their bulls in the back hills. There was no joking today, there was no humor or energy, we didn't function much as a team, just 4 individuals who knew their jobs. While the people didn't seem even to notice that the horses were gone, we horses certainly noticed that our friends were missing.

May 8

Today I took my person's grandson for a ride out in the fields. He's 4 and growing up fast. My people trust me with him and I make sure that I take extra special care of him, he's very small. He hasn't grown to be like my owner yet, he's gentle and kind and kisses my nose. The old man still gave me a harsh warning in the barn, before I was brought out all tacked up for my tiny charge. I only understood part of the words that were said, but his body language said more than enough. Everything I needed to hear in that threat was communicated through the tobacco and bourbon breath, and through the tension in the old man's shoulders. I would be beat within an inch of my life if I dropped that little boy.

I had no intention of dropping him. I have never intended to drop anyone. The old man coming off my back because he made a mistake is not my fault, even if I was often times blamed for the human ignorance and ego.

This boy is precious and I am especially fond of him. I took him all over the field, and figured out pretty quickly that he had no idea what to do with the reins or the bit, but when he pointed in a certain direction I could feel him move on my back. I would follow where he pointed, more so follow the direction he shifted to. He thought it was great fun and giggled and would holler "Come on Lady! That way!" while he pointed and off we would go.

After our ride was over, my owner, the old man seemed irritated with me. He was saying how a good horse shouldn't be going off the pointing of a rider. But I wasn't going off the little guy pointing! I was going off his seat- the same as I do for you old man! That's why you look so good riding me! That's why it looks so easy, because I get there off your seat before you even get to yanking on my face! It's been many years and for some reason I always assume that they will learn- but I guess they never do.

May 16

My people brought 2 new horses into the herd yesterday, they are both just young kids- "Red," a cocky 4 year old and a little horse named "Ben" that's about 8. They seem to be good horses. Ben is wise for his age, and cautious. Red seems more like a learn on the job kind of kid, lots of ego with little real sense. They both seem generally good minded though and eager to please. Red calls me grandma, and my owner seems to have taken a shine to him for working the pastures. They were out early this morning and I guess Red hasn't been working very long because the old man got after him pretty bad.
"What the heck is wrong with that old man, I didn't do anything to deserve getting hit." Red quietly enquired while he rubbed his bruised cheek on the inside of his front leg.
"That's just him. He doesn't accept mistakes, disobedience or fear. You get use to it. It's just the way he is. He is a fierce warrior. You have to learn to pay really close attention and read his seat, know where he wants to go before he goes that way. You'll get it."
I was a little sad that I wasn't taken, that use to be my patrol, but all in all I was glad for the day off.

May 23

The grandkids were here again this week. My people have had me up
in a stall the past few days and when I heard them pull up I got
excited for the opportunity to be out and tote the little guy around
again. I was dancing a little in my stall, with anticipation. My owner
came in looked at me and just shook his head. He continued walking
down the line. Ben was chosen to be the lucky one entrusted with the
baby. Everyone seemed so excited and I heard one of the people say
that Ben was a gift for the little boy.

I heard my owner's gruff voice, "Tucker won't have to ride that old
nag anymore. She's too old to be of much interest. Ben will be able to
keep up. Tuker can start learning the ropes around here."
This made me sad, I was a little surprised; It's not that I can't keep
up, I was just trying to be careful with the precious little boy that
they had entrusted to me. I know what the consequences are for
dropping a rider, and the implications for dropping that child were
made very clear. Ben and Tucker are both young, I hope they take
care of eachother.

May 25

My owner's wife came out and brushed me today, she often sneaks
me carrots from the garden or apples from the orchard. She has
always been kind to me, for the most part. It is rare that she rides,
usually she is in charge of cooking and cleaning for the owner and the
ranch hands. These are the moments that I love the most, she comes
out and brushes me, gives me scratches, sometimes she braids my
mane and tail. When she braids my mane and tail, my owner gets

angry at us both, but the woman has a way with him, "Well, I think she looks nice!" She gives me a pat and looks over at me softly, "dontcha girl?" There is always a wry smile attached to the end of that same conversation and it's my job to huff a little and nose for a carrot. My owner just gruffs and takes me away to work. He is always a little rougher with me on the days when his wife gives me attention, but I don't mind, because it's worth the carrots and kindness from his woman.

June 5

They don't do much with me anymore. I don't work the morning run, and I just sit here in the stall. They come by and feed me, fill my water, but even when the farrier came out I got left and my feet are getting a little sore- maybe they just forgot? They will remember me, I know they will.

I would get left sometimes when we were out in the pasture, I would get nervous and run they said I was "hard to catch" but they are always so rough with me and I just get anxious. I was always good at my job and though I can sometimes be hard as far as the people are concerned, I have never intentionally hurt one of them, even when I was a baby, it was just because I was nervous.

They'll remember me next time.

June 6

I heard my people talking tonight about loading the trailer and going somewhere. I didn't catch all of the conversation, but I'm excited.

Usually that means that we have to bring the cattle down from the mountains and that's a hard job. It's been my job forever and I'm the best one here. You don't send the 4 year old to do a seasoned hand's work. It'll likely be that Red comes along to learn and help, but my owner and I will be the ones that head over the mountain through the pass and guide the cows around. It's one of my favorite jobs when the season starts to turn. I wish Duke and Sally could be here, we were always the best team for these types of jobs. It's a hard few days of work, but you can't beat the prairie grass and that river water; so cold, so sweet, it's not trough water that's for sure.

I knew they wouldn't forget me. I need to get some good sleep tonight so that I am ready to work in the morning. I do wish my feet had gotten done, but the long stuff will break off on the rock beds, We've run this before, might even be good that my feet aren't done, they are a little sore, but they aren't as tender as just after a trim. This is good. This will be good.

Chapter 2: The Auction House

I had spent my life dedicated to working, raising my children, raising my owner's children, training new horses in our ways, and tending to my work. My past had it's good days and it's rough days, but I am a strong horse with a sharp mind. Even when I was sore I gave my all and tried not to show that I was off on any given day. I worked alongside my equine and human partners and while I would occasionally run or shy from being caught, I was praised in the valley as being the best at what I did. I am wary of people I don't know, hell I was somewhat wary of the people who owned me. But strangers make me nervous. I'm not sure what I have done wrong, that my owners brought me here; calves haven't even finished hitting the ground and there is work to be done.
I was a good horse.

Auction houses are the number one place that kill buyers acquire horses. It is the first dumping site for the domesticated horse and the transition to death row for many.

June 7

I'm nervous here, I am not sure what is going on. My people brought
me here and left. I thought we were going to work, but I have never
worked in a place like this. My people are not here. I don't know
when my people are coming back, if they are coming back. A man I
do not know put me in this space with a bunch of other horses.
Some of them are injured, some are skinny, some seem fine, but
everyone is a bit on edge. Some of the other horses are yelling for
their friends who don't seem to be here. Some of the horses are
yelling for their people, they don't seem to be here either.

I am in a pen with 14 other horses including a momma and baby that
try to keep to themselves as best they can. I tried to find out her
name, but she just kept running away to find another corner. I can't
say that I blame her, I am doing pretty much the same thing in this
pen. I have never been in such an environment. There is a lot of
pushing and shoving and I have had my shoulder slammed twice.
There is a big gelding that seems to run this pen, he is fat and mean
and pins his ears at everyone, kicking and making a fuss. He struck at
me once and I turned my butt to him and gave him a solid wallop,
but he's just angry all the time. He acts like a stallion. The only time
his ears perk up is when a person comes through and looks around.
Apparently this boy has never really been around other horses before,
or at least that is the impression that I am getting.

I am not use to this chaos. I worked years and have never seen a place
like this. This can't be normal. What about my herd? What am I
supposed to do now? This doesn't seem right. I can smell cattle, but
.they are not within view. Maybe we are all here to work? It doesn't

seem that way, but I don't know what else to think. I am a horse, work is what I do, is what I have always done. This place smells of anxiety and fear. Some of the horses are calm, but a lot of them are just here, not knowing what will happen next.

There is a man who comes through every few hours and stares at us. I suppose they are checking the horses. We had a ranch hand that was in charge of checking the pastures during the day and another one during the night in case there was something wrong with one of us. This seems to be the same. The ranch hands were always friendly and had their favorite horses that they talked to, or would sneak treats to. This man is not like that, he doesn't talk to the horses, or pet them. He seems cold to me. While he doesn't appear to be mean towards anyone, he doesn't seem to know or have a personal relationship with any of the horses here, either. He just stares into the paddocks and pastures, looks over each one of us and then moves on.

June 8

None of the horses here seem to work. I haven't seen anyone pulled out yet and ridden or tacked up for working, we all just stand around. I don't know when my people are coming back, I miss my herd and I miss my people, even the mean old man. I just don't like it here. I am afraid here. I want to go home.

I know that people can be harsh, and these are strangers, I don't like strangers. Maybe this is a place just for horses. Maybe they just feed us and leave us alone, but I fear that is not the case. There seems to be too much tension here for that. I am trying to just mind my own business and stay out of the way, in a corner until I figure this out.

It's difficult though, all of the chaos and noise makes that nearly impossible.

The man who put me in this pen came last night and this morning and fed everyone. He didn't talk to any of us, he didn't touch any of us, he just fed us and left. I can't seem to get my head on straight. There is just too much going on, yet at the same time nothing is happening. It's confusing. Trying to lie down and sleep was nearly impossible, everyone was vying for a spot. I looked to the momma and baby, the foal was lying underneath the mare, she was protecting him as best she could. I can see that she is very nervous and not handled much, she and the foal run when the man comes through.

There was a lot of chaos when the man brought food, the skinnier horses were pushed off, and while I am a solid girl I couldn't make my way to the food because there was just too much kicking, screaming and general battle for position. The ones that got to the hay wouldn't let any of the rest of us in to eat. Myself and one of the skinny girls managed to get in towards the end and clean up the scraps out of the dirt...but I am hungry. The skinny and I didn't talk, she mostly used me as a shield and squeezed up against me to get in and help clean up the little bit of hay that was left.

I am use to fighting with people, I am not use to fighting with other horses. Where I lived before we all worked, some of us worked the fields, some of us carried people around, we all shared the food and the labor. Even those of us that weren't friends got along, because we all had a respect of one another, we were all there to do a job, same as the people. But here, no one seems to have a job and there doesn't seem to be much in the way of respect for one another. Everyone is from a different place. Where did all of these horses come from?

There is a quarter horse that seems well acclimated. He's a dun and looks like he works regularly, he's wide and fit. He is in one pen over, but he comes over and chats at the pretty girls in my pen. He seems cordial, and he is calmer than most of the other horses here, so I asked him questions about this place.

"Excuse me, uh, sir?" I stuttered.

The dun looked at me with surprise, he had been chatting up a pretty flaxen in my pen and apparently was unaware of my existence. "Yes, ma'am? What can I do ya fer?"

"What is this place? I have never been anywhere like it."

The dun looked shocked, "Really? Well firstly, my name is Mac. This place is an auction house. I have personally been to three of them before. They are pretty straight forward. We hang around in these pens for a while, some of the horses are in stalls." Mac motioned with his head towards a row of stalls. "But the gist is the same. We hang out. After a few days we get ridden, walked or pushed through a little parade in front of a lot of people. It's noisy and everyone is yelling. But it's simple enough. They move us around in a little pen and show us off. At the end of our time in the parade we go back to the pens or to stalls." He paused to make eyes at one of the palomino mares in one of the other pens. She proceeded to ignore him, and then continued, "after the parade either the same day or sometime the next day, we go to work for new folks. It's a pretty good gig. So we work for them for awhile and then we come back to the auction house and the process starts all over again."

"Well, how long do we work for the new people? What kind of work?"

He thought for a minute, "It varies. I worked for my last owner for 2 years, the one before that for about 6 months. My first owner, I worked for him for 5 years. I have always done the same work, branding calves, checking fences, roping calves. Always the same work, just with different partners." With that he trotted off, showing interest in one of the roan mares in his own pen. He doesn't seem bothered by this, and it doesn't sound all that bad. But something doesn't seem right to me about what he said, one thing that doesn't make much sense to me. I am 22, I have never been to one of these places before. I just don't know, but at least for now, it seems I have made a friend.

Mac's Journal:

An old mare approached me today, she seems nervous. Unsure of the auction house and of people in general. She was enquiring about this place and what goes on here. I explained the best that I could, but I don't know that it made sense to her- she seems lost.

My most recent human brought me in this morning, sometimes things just don't work out or aren't a right fit. He was nice enough and we got along okay, but we just didn't fit quite right, I suppose. I will try to impress the people at the parade tomorrow, I have to be at the top of my game. As long as I have a job to do, I think things will work out okay.

I hope that poor old girl finds somewhere to give her some lighter work though, it doesn't seem like she's going to do well with just anyone. She is built right for it, but it seems like her hind leg is just a little stiff. She's an older gal, she doesn't need to be doing rough work. I forgot to get her name. In any case, I am looking forward to whatever new adventure

awaits. Until then maybe I can find a nice little mare to hang out with.
I like the mares a lot better than the geldings in here, who wants to
hang out with boys all day when there so many pretty girls here?

June 10

I watched as they saddled Mac and left him tied to a post for a while.
There was a different man here today, and I watched closely as he
brushed Mac and tacked him up, it didn't seem too bad. After a
while they took Mac away, he was gone for about 10 minutes. When
they brought him back out he seemed pleased with himself, and went
into one of the stalls. The man pat him on the neck and told him
"good boy." That was it. I've never seen that before. It was odd.

Some of the other horses went through the parade with saddles and
tack, some went through with just a halter on. One big mare was all
tacked out in driving gear without a cart and ground driven through.
The man that came in to halter me was moving fast, I got scared and
ran away. He came at me again and his body language was suggestive
of his irritation. I just knew he was going to hit me so I kept running-
and he left. I was convinced that I had managed to avoid the beating
today. There were about 15 of us in this pen this morning, by the
afternoon there were only 5 of us, three of us successfully avoided the
beating that we knew was coming, but the mom and baby in here too
were spooked hard and the good old girl was just protecting her little
one.

When it came time for the parade that Mac had talked about. The
man that was so nice to Mac came in with a noisy thing on the end of
a stick and bout scared the crap out of the lot of us. We all went

together through the parade- he ran us down a little alleyway and through a door. Once we got in there it was just as Mac had described, mostly. It was noisy and confusing, there was yelling and hollering and a lot of movement, the five us us were are packed together- I hadn't expected a space this small; somewhere in the chaos the little one got stepped on. It seemed like it took forever, but looking back it was maybe a few minutes.

We are in a different pen now, all five of us. This pen has about 12 or 15 horses in it, I recognize 3 of them besides the five I came in with. The three I recognize were in the pen with us before. The baby is limping badly and there is an old man in with us that doesn't seem to be doing too well, he is very skinny and his eye doesn't look good. He probably use to be black, but now is a dingy grey, his age showing hard across his face. Even with his swollen and goopy eye, he seems sharp as a tack. I bet he was impressive as a young horse. I went over to him and asked his name.

He turned his head to look at me out of his good eye. "Bert. Why do you ask, miss?"

"Miss? Sir I am twenty two years old! I have not been a 'miss' in many years."

He huffed, "Well, I'm 31 and am old enough to be your father." He had tickled himself and was laughing and coughing all at the same time. I got the impression that besides being old, skinny and injured, he was probably sick.

Bert, myself, and the momma with a baby all huddled together, not because we were close or even liked each other, but because it gave us a fighting chance at getting a meal. Myself being the only one with any good weight on my bones, sort of became the shield for our makeshift herd during feeding time, and I was able to be a wall for the others so they could eat, at least for a while.

Mac said that we go work for new people now- I am not sure what to expect. I can work, I am very good at working, but that old man with the bad eye- what kind of work is he going to do? He would need a lot of hay and a vet before he could even think of working. That baby is going to need a vet too. I think out of the group of us here, there are probably 6 horses that look like we are even able to work. Mac was ridden in the parade, we were pushed through with a flappy stick. I am questioning whether Mac has the same experience as other horses or if it's just because they know him.

Mac's Journal

I did my thing, I walked, trotted, cantered in that tiny parade. I did spins and stops and never once did the bit move. All in anticipating the legs. I am fit and know my stuff. Sounded like I went for a good number this time, 2500 ain't bad for a ranch working machine! I am excited to start with my new human partner, to meet the new crew and proceed with this page in my life. They put me in a stall after the parade instead of back in the pen this time, so I can't ask Grandma what her name is. But I watched when they tried to go in and get her for the parade. I was surprised, she's pretty quick and agile for an old lady. I wonder if she's a ranch horse. I remember thinking she would be good on a cow. They got the flag out and pushed her through with the other horses that don't catch. I never really understood that. Why don't they just stick their head in the halter? It's just a person, people are mostly good, right? I know Grandma is a little nervous but I wasn't expecting that. There is a man headed in my direction with a halter, that must be my new partner. He's built as sturdy as I am, but he has a soft eye. I think this one will be nice to work with. I'm on my way. Good luck Grandma.

Chapter 3: The Pens

The kill pens are death row for horses. You are fed, watered and wait for the day that your number comes up. Where inmates in prison can wait years for an execution date, horses typically wait in hours, days and weeks. Prisoners sentenced to death are treated humanely, they are taken on an individual basis, put to sleep and receive injections which cause their death, these people who have done horrendous harm to their human victims.

Horses are not treated with such kindness. They are packed onto trailers, with animals pushing shoving and injuring themselves, injuring one another in fear and anxiety. They are transported to facilities where, if they are lucky, they receive a gun (in the form of a bolt gun) to the head, and then their throats are slit. If they are one of the unlucky ones, they are tortured, abused and then slaughtered in a violent death. Most of them being punished for what? They meet a violent end for their dedication to humanity and are discarded as trash. We, as humans treat these animals (which most have done no harm), exceedingly worse, than the animals of our own species that thrive on torture and violence.

Those who are rescued are few, compared to the multitudes we send to their deaths for our convenience every year.

June 11

Early this morning, all of us were loaded on to one big trailer. They didn't even bother to halter anyone they just pushed us down a narrow alley and smashed us all into the same trailer. It should probably be hauling only half the horses that are in here. During the ride to this new place there was a lot of shoving, kicking, biting, and anxiety. The little baby got stepped on again and the momma got scraped up trying to protect her little one. It was compacted chaos. The old man got banged up pretty good, but I did my best to keep myself between those three and the rest of the chaos. I got kicked once and stomped my foot hard hollering at everyone to just settle down. It was my mad mare voice and things settled after a few minutes. The drive wasn't very long, thank goodness.

This new place seems a little like the one we just left, maybe it's a new auction house, I don't know. There are a lot of horses here though, far more than were at the last auction house and these horses are more varied in color type and size than I have ever seen, nonetheless all in one place.

I miss my herd back home. I miss Duke.

Mac's Journal

I got to the new place, it's a large ranch, there are other horses and the food is good. I came in with another horse, he's younger and seems a little bit shy, but I will show him the ropes, he'll be okay. I heard the woman talking this morning, looks like we are headed over the mountain tomorrow to bring the cows in from the winter pasture. It smells like a good time. I am eager to get to work. The drive was a long one, but it was nice. There is a big barn and irrigated fields. All in all I think there are probably 6 horses here. I saw a number of ranch hands too, so looks like it will be an awesome place to work. A young kid, maybe 14 came out to greet us when we pulled up. Once we were unloaded into stalls he asked the man who bought me, if I was his new horse. My new owner said, "Yep, just give me a few weeks to get a handle on him, break him in a little bit." They boy came over and hugged me around the neck, and then dutifully followed the man out of the barn. I am pumped. This will be my first child to tend to.

June 13

There was a trailer here this morning, they loaded about twenty horses onto it including the old man with the bad eye, I hope he makes it safely to where ever he is headed. I overheard one of the people call him a "direct ship." One of the mares across the way said that he was on the truck to Canada, I have no idea where that is, but I hope it's nice for the old guy. I tried to ask the mare what that was, but she just walked away, with a look of defeat to her.

Today was the first time that I really had a chance to take in this place. There are a lot of us here! Everything from pregnant mares with new babies, babies by themselves, big horses, ponies, donkeys. Every age, shape and size imaginable. Seems like there is a little bit of everything in these pens. Mac said that we work for our new owners now, but I don't really understand. What kind of work are those babies going to do? The oldest of them in the far pen, is not more than 6 months old, with most of them looking more like 3 months old. There are skinny and lame horses here in vast numbers. What on earth could they possibly do? I don't think Mac was right. I don't think we work, but if that is the case then what *do* we do here?

I don't care for people, I never know what to expect. It never seemed to matter how hard I worked or how much I hurt, I was going to get beat either way. The people here don't really seem to notice me much, and I am at least grateful for that- I try to just avoid them. They don't really seem to handle any of the horses though, they just load them onto trailers and out they go, or unload them off of trailers and in they come. The horses get a sticker with a number on their butt and put in a pen. I have a sticker too.

Sherry's Journal

Tomorrow Joe and I will head back out to the kill pens. It's always a long trip and fills me with conflict. There are so many horses. How can I possibly make a difference? Joe says that we save the ones we can, but it will never be enough, really. They are all such beautiful souls. I hate that I can't save them all. They all deserve to be saved. We try to save more than we can even accommodate at the rescue. We fundraise, advertise and try to post them on social media hoping that someone out there will adopt a horse that is waiting at death's door. We try so hard, only to see those beautiful animals loaded onto trailers and taken to their death.

Sometimes it feels like I don't make a difference at all, but maybe I can make a difference for some. It is a heartbreaking passion that we have, the love of rescue.

June 14

There were two people here today who were going around the pens. A woman and a man. The woman was older, but still strong. She was lean, but muscular with long dark hair that had just begun to grey. The man was tall and wiry with short blonde hair. They pulled a couple of horses out and had a man ride them around. They took some pictures and then put the horses back. They didn't act normal for people. It was odd. I watched everything they did, every move. When they came to my pen, I tried to hide in the corner. But then I heard the woman say my name, so I looked up.

"Lady, 22 years old. This says that she ships on the truck coming Monday. According to the note here, she is broke to ride, she was a ranch horse. Get some pictures and we will see about getting a riding video."

They took a couple of pictures and made some noises, clicking and kissing. They tried to call me over- but I know better. There's always some ulterior motive when it comes to people and I simply can't bring myself to go to strangers.

A man came in, I tried to run, but there just wasn't that much room to move around. I tried to hide in the corner and pick my head way up high, but he blocked all of my escape routes and he got a halter on me. So I just braced, I was waiting for the beating, that first punch that always comes when they finally catch me. I had my eyes shut and I just tightened up, but then he just tugged on the halter for me to follow him. I gave in, as I am trained to do. I was just too tired at that point.

They didn't put a saddle on me, the guy just climbed onto a fence and hopped onto my back. I did my best to do what he wanted, but he had those shoe spikes on and kept bumping me in the ribs and pulling my head around. Those other two people were there, taking pictures and whatever a video is, I suppose. They were talking back and forth with the guy on my back, about me. I only caught part of what they were saying because I was thinking about something else, somewhere else. After a while the man put me back in the pen.

What the hell was that all about, and why did that woman know my name?

I lived at the same place for 21 of my 22 years, but in the last 2 weeks, I have lived in 3 different places. This is all so confusing. Where are the cattle, where is the work? All I have seen in the past few days are horses, and a good portion of those are messed up horses, though there are some really nice solid looking horses here too. What the hell is going on?

Sherry's Journal
There were more new horses in the pens today. It's just so heartbreaking, I don't think anyone will ever really know how hard this all is. To know that we can save only a fraction of the horses here. An older mare, Lady, was hiding in the corner. We were able to get pictures of her and of 28 other horses, with the hope that someone out there will adopt one of these horses, or donate to buy them some time, or help us rescue them. I spent the evening listing them all on social media channels, with bios and information that we have. I hate that some of the people at the pens are so forward with the horses there. Poor Lady was scared to death, but settled after she was

caught. I am glad that the people at the pens at least give us the chance to try and help some of these horses, many of the kill pens don't. It's truly the most heartbreaking part of what we do.

June 15

Today was quiet. Well, as quiet as it gets around here anyway. More horses left, but I didn't really notice- I was daydreaming mostly. Thinking back to when I was just a foal, running, playing, just being a kid. I was trying to remember a time before people. I must have been too small to remember really, because people have always been there. I remember they called me stubborn and hot when I was a kid. I was pretty small the first time I can remember kicking one of them; he was trying to take my legs out from under me, I got scared and I kicked him. He kneed me in the belly and knocked the wind out of me, then I got shoved into a corner and they went through and picked up each of my feet. I fought them the best I could back then, but I always remembered after that; they can smell your fear and they'll use it against you. I have been wary of them ever since.

June 20

A new load of horses came in today and those two people were back again, taking pictures. They said something about an extension. I'm not really sure what their deal is, or why they keep showing up. They don't seem to do much. They stopped by my pen and tried to coax me over, but I just ignored them, nobody tried to get on me or catch me today. I'm thankful for that.

I'm feeling kind of down today, everything is just kind of a blur. There doesn't seem much point in making any friends here, horses come and go- from what I hear in peripheral conversations there isn't a single horse that has been here longer than a month. That seems suspect to me, but I guess that is how things go now. This auction house seems different though- there aren't a lot of people, or the parades, just the trucks loaded with horses, coming and going.

June 21

A new load of horses came in today, big horses. They call themselves the PMU mares. They seem like an odd herd. It's as though they all know each other, but not really together. Three of them got put in the pen next to mine. A big old chestnut mare came and stood by my corner. She called me Grandma. She was asking me what this place is. I told her to go ask one of the other horses, I didn't even lift my head. This big PMU nosed me over the fence. "Grandma!" She insisted. I picked my head up and said, "What?!"
She was looking around frantically, on edge. "What the hell is this place? Why aren't there any tubes or bags? Why aren't any of the horses tied? Can we lay down?" I realized this mare was terrified, and as the man came around to check paddocks, she pinned her ears. She was as untrusting as I am, more so maybe.

"I don't know what this place is. I think it's an auction house, but it's not like the last one that I was in. I don't know anything about any tubes or bags, I haven't seen any, and yes I suppose if you wanted to- you could lay down. What's your name honey?" She said that they called her "236." All I could think was, well that's an odd name for a horse.

I asked her what a PMU is, I had never heard of that breed before. I was not prepared for the answer that I got. We spoke for a long time, and while I don't know that we would qualify as friends, but perhaps temporary companions in this place.

236's Journal

Eight of us were loaded onto a trailer today and brought to a strange place. None of the horses here are tied, they don't have catheters, and as far as I can tell most of them seen not to be pregnant. The eight of us that came here, "didn't take" this past breeding, which makes us useless. I can't even remember how long it has been since I wasn't pregnant...or tied...or peed without a tube inserted. It's like heaven here. We get fed, and for the first time in I don't even know how long, I laid down. I didn't want to get up, but the monsters brought us hay and I was hungry after a long rest. Horses are fighting over getting to the feed, but I am a big girl and just shoved my way through the commotion.

I met an old grandma horse next door- she seems tired, but there's a fire in her that I like. She doesn't like the monsters either. She asked me what breed a PMU is, and I explained to her that we aren't a breed- we're a factory.

I am a Premarin Mare, I spent my life up to this point pregnant, so they could harvest my urine, for people to ingest. They call it "medicine" but honestly who tortures horses and drinks their urine for medicine? That seems barbaric...it is barbaric. A lot of horses call them "people", maybe that is a different word for monster.
We are bred as soon as our first heat arrives and we are kept pregnant, they take our babies away, the girls sometimes follow our plight,

destined to be kept pregnant for their lives, standing in stalls, not able to move about or lay down. The colts are killed or sent away immediately once we are confirmed in foal again. I have had 8 boys and 4 girls, they were all such beautiful children. I am 14 years old, the eighteenth foal from my mother. My last colt was a beautiful boy, I could hear him calling for me until he couldn't call anymore.

June 22

Those two weird people were back again. 236 stayed close to my fence, and we both watched them warily. They keep talking to me. They pointed their little camera at me again and were talking the whole time. They called me "shut down" and were blabbing about something when I started to listen a little more carefully. Something about "rescue", "kill pen", and "slaughter bound." I don't know what a rescue or a kill pen is, but I know what slaughter is, they use to do it to the turkeys and the pigs on the farm.

Is that what this is? Are we going to be slaughtered?
I don't understand...why?

I worked for that mean old cuss for most of my life!! I carried him around in blazing heat, bone freezing cold, helped with the cows, toted his kids and his grandkids around. And now I'm to die?! Why?

I know I have slowed down a little, but only a little. I'm a little greyer than I once was, and I can be hard to catch, but you really can't blame me for that. I always worked hard, gave my all, and tried to do my best. And I almost never defended myself when you were harsh, or when you hurt me, hell at least not since I was a kid, I only run away or try to avoid the beating. What have I done to earn death, why am I to be slaughtered? This doesn't make any sense!

They seemed to be taking pictures of 236 also. So I warned her to be careful. I didn't tell her about what slaughter meant, I need to think.

236's Journal

There were monsters here today, that I haven't seen before. They were taking pictures of some of the horses, pulling some of them out and getting on them. They had some sort of list they were going off of, it looked like one of the inventory lists from the factory I was in. That's all horses are to the monsters- inventory.

Grandma seemed very upset by them, she was very nervous and tried hard to shove herself deeper into the corner of her pen. I stood guard over her as best I could. She seemed triggered by something they had said, but I don't know what it was, maybe I will ask her tomorrow. Tonight she was in a world of her own, like her mind was spinning. I have seen that look on some of the mares at the factory, before they collapse from exhaustion and from not being able to sleep. At least we get to sleep in this place, we get to lay down and sleep.

Sherry's Journal
The old bay mare, Lady, is looking worse and worse. She has lost weight and is shut down. I worry for her. Three of the horses that we listed were given a reprieve. It's not enough, they aren't saved yet, their death is just postponed to buy us more time to get them saved.. My heart breaks knowing that the trailer will be there soon. Perhaps I will go out and spend some time with the rescues in the pasture for

a bit, they always bring me back to why I do this. It doesn't look like I will be sleeping tonight, anyhow.

June 23

I guess I have come to terms. I was looking around at all the horses in this place, so many souls....lost. Just the sheer numbers were overwhelming to me. I was trying to think of how many horses I had seen leave, just in the few days that I have been here, but I can't remember. Dozens? Hundreds? So many souls here only to die. And then I remembered the old horse Bert, and everything in me just dropped into a darkness.

Please, no. Not that sweet old guy. I didn't want to think of it, but I couldn't avoid it. I know how they slaughtered the turkeys at the farm, and then I pictured the horrifying scene played out on that sweet old horse with the bad eye, and hope simply drained out of me.

I knew humans couldn't be trusted.

June 24

Those people were back saying something about being nearly there. Where? I'm here, and like the rest of these poor souls, soon I will be on someone's plate. They were talking to each other about how I didn't look good. They said that it looked like 236 and I were bonding. What else was I going to do in this death trap? Yes I found comfort in another horse destined for hell!

All I could think was, "Fine!! Eat something else then!!!"

But I didn't move, I just stayed in my corner and looked at the ground- I don't even want to look at these people anymore. I gave my life to you humans, I worked my whole life for you, and now you will take my very last breath.

I give up.

Mac's Journal

I should have seen it. We were working and this man that I have been working with is a really good guy, we work well together. We were trotting along checking the fences in the pasture with mares and babies. I should have seen it, but I didn't. I hit that hole and my leg popped, there was blinding pain and I went down. I tried to keep my human partner safe, and he made it clear of me before I went down.

We were about an hour ride from the barn. But my partner asked me up, so I limped on and carried us both back to the barn. My leg is pretty swollen and it doesn't look good. They gave me something for the pain and assured me that the vet would be out tomorrow to take a look at it.

Sherry's Journal

The fundraising for Lady and the PMU mare that is in the next pen over has covered part of the cost to get them out. I will have to dip into my savings if it doesn't end up fully covering our needs for them, but we **will** get them out and to safety.

June 27

The past few days have all just run together. It's been one big numb
blur. 236 acts like she wants to ask me a question, but always seems
to stop herself. Today was different, more real, more painful.

A truck came in with ten horses, one of those horses was Mac. I
called to him, and in his usual way he hollered back cordially. He
didn't look good, apparently he hurt his leg really bad, something
about a break and a tear (I am not sure he was too far away for me to
catch it all when he hollered back). He stepped in a hole, when he
and his person were out checking fences. That was a few days ago. He
looked like he was in a lot of pain, a little sucked up but trying to be
strong.

.

A truck left today, they were one short. So they took "that lame
dun." I couldn't bring myself to tell him, or warn him or even speak.
It all happened so fast and then he was gone. Loaded onto the last
ride he will ever take.

Goodbye Mac.

Mac's Journal

*My owner loaded me up in a trailer today and took me to a new
auction house. I was sad to see that place go- I thought it was a nice place
to work and I was so looking forward to working with the young boy.
My leg is swollen and looks nasty, the pain is barely manageable. The
vet said that I broke something and that there was a tear in the tendon,
he said the down time would be long. I suppose the people of that ranch*

couldn't keep me for that long not working, I get it though- work has to get done.

I saw that old mare at the auction house. She called to me and we spoke for a moment before I was loaded back up onto this new trailer. The ride has been a long one so far, my leg is hurting and is badly swollen. Hopefully the new place will be as good as the last.
Oh, we just pulled in!
I hear horses screaming.

It smells like death.

June 28

I couldn't sleep last night. Mac was heavy on my mind and it took me back to my home ranch. I wonder how Ben is doing with his new little charge. I hope they are okay. I remember the first time that I was entrusted with my person's son, Thomas. I guess he was about 14 at the time, I was about 5 and thought I was something special. They called me "hot" but I just had a lot of energy and wanted to work. We were out checking fences, there were three of us. If I remember correctly it was me, Duke and Sally.

Thomas had a heavy hand, was pretty rough on my mouth, and hard on my sides- it was his first time out running the fences on me. By 8:30 it was already starting to get hot out and Thomas yanked on my face to bring me around and I came around a little too fast (faster than I probably should have) and Thomas came off.

"Set her straight!" his father told him, that was always the line before the beating--set her straight. He knew I hadn't done anything wrong, but the fault would be held by me nonetheless. That man-child coming off of me, wasn't my fault. But I decided that day that they would have to earn every inch of me, I wouldn't just give them the trust, they were going to have to earn it. It wasn't the worst beating I ever got, but something in me turned that day. That was when I started running, they would have to work to catch me. I wasn't going to be violent, it's not in me to do it, but they would still have to earn their work horse every day.

I had made it a point to be the best working horse on that ranch, and they praised my working ability to everyone that would come out for the brandings. They use to laugh and tell their friends, "If you can catch her, there's not one better!"

I was the best. I hope Mac doesn't suffer long.

236 Journal

Grandma doesn't look good at all, she hasn't eaten and is getting skinny, she has worn hard in the past few days and I am concerned for her. I like to think that we are friends, but she has been quiet.

She recognized a horse that came in a couple days ago, they loaded him onto another trailer pretty quickly. Grandma shut down pretty hard after that and hasn't eaten since. I don't think the trailers that leave here are good for the horses on them. Tomorrow I will talk to Grandma and try to get her to eat something. I have never had a friend before, so I am not sure what to do, but I will do what I can for the old girl.

June 30

Those weird people were back today, they seemed excited...maybe they were hungry. There was another man with them this time. The man who usually comes around to feed us was busy pushing about 20 horses onto another death trailer. I thought I had one good fight left in me and they were going to have to earn this meal.

The woman approached me with a halter and I ran to the other end of the pen. It took about 20 minutes for them to catch me. It wasn't much of a fight, I'm just too tired. The third man must have been a vet, because he gave me a shot and took some blood. The woman tried to touch my neck, I just tensed. I'm always tense with people now... unpredictable beasts.

The vet said I needed my feet and my teeth done. Really? You guys are going to eat me and you're worried about my feet and my teeth? They are sore though, it's been a long time. I am getting more confused by the day. This doesn't make any sense to me at all.

They did the same thing to 236, though she had a little more fight in her than I did. I was proud of her, she put that woman in the mud! But the vet gave her a shot that made her drunk and sleepy, they took her blood and then let her go.

Why are they taking blood? Maybe that is how they judge how good we taste. I don't remember seeing them taking blood on the horses before. They didn't take blood on Mac...oh Mac, I'm so sorry.

When 236 came out of her drunken stupor she was insistent that I eat something, insistent that we talk about what is going on in this place. She was half concerned, half angry. So I told her everything that I know.

236's Journal

Those monsters caught and doped me! I fought them, but they were quick with the needle. I finally convinced Grandma to eat some food, and I pushed her until she talked. I thought I wanted to know what this place is, I was wrong.

This place, which is more like heaven than the place I had known my whole life, is in fact, just a different hell. Another phase of the monsters' self indulgent, torturous nature. They keep us trapped in tiny standing stalls for years on end, not allowed to sleep, kept pregnant with tubes in our hind ends, harvesting our pee and then ship us off to the death traps.

We horses are feeling, thinking; we give the monsters every ounce of ourselves and they just use us up, abuse us and destroy us. I have resigned myself to look out for Grandma. I have resigned myself to teach them that this meal will fight back.

Sherry's Journal

The fundraising for Lady and her PMU friend has come through, along with 2 other horses. Today we went out to get a blood draw on both mares and were just about killed. Joe and I are both sore this evening. Lady was hard to catch, but settled down more than I had thought she would have, once caught. The PMU mare, 236 is simply terrified of everything and knocked me down, I thought she was going to get aggressive but she proceeded to just hide in the corner. The vet got in there and sedated her before she could do much more. My heart just breaks for her, Once the coggins and bloodwork go through we will be able to bring them home to get them out of that hell hole. Hopefully she will settle a bit.

Chapter 4: Quarantine

Rescues do not always take in the horses that they think will be easy to rehabilitate. Often, they take in the horses they can, and the horses that need. While each life lost to the horse meat trade is a horrendous loss to the heart of those who fight for them, each horse saved is viewed as inherently worthy of life.

It is a passion of endless work, heartbreak and hope. The majority of horse rescues depend on donations and volunteers to make a difference and are criticized for those they cannot save, whether because of space or funding. Dumping horses is an epidemic.

Our horse rescues and sanctuaries, and the people behind them work tirelessly and passionately to dress the wounds which society and the horse industry have created. Quarantine, in most cases includes vet cots, transport costs, farrier costs, time, feed, effort and things that cannot be measured in dollars, but nonetheless take dollars to make happen. Every rescue knows the pain of heartbreak, and the beauty of those that are brought in and rescued from the slaughter pipeline. And while not every horse learns to trust, every horse deserves the opportunity for a second chance.

July 1

Those two people came super early this morning, it must have been about 5am. When they came into my pen, 236 went crazy and tried to bite the man from over the fence. She called and yelled at them, things that I can't bring myself to repeat. The man who feeds us singled her out and while he kept his distance, he pushed her forward into a stall. The two strange people sedated her, they were quick and skilled. I tried to call and warn her, but I was too late and she was so drunk from the shot that she could barely lift her head. They loaded her first, onto the trailer. Then they came for me. And this old girl decided to give it all she had. I managed to kick the man, but it was a grazing shot and I didn't see when the woman came around and got the lead rope around my neck. I instinctively accepted the halter, as I had done every time for the past twenty something years. They loaded me onto the trailer next to 236, with two other horses from the death pens.

The ride was a solemn one. I had resigned myself to be caught, and to die. I had seen so many go over the past few weeks. The old man Bert, Mac, the old girl and her little baby. So many horses. I don't understand these humans, but I guess I was just glad that I didn't have to wait anymore. It was my turn for death, and to a point, I welcomed it.

The other horses in the trailer seemed to have a similar mindset, we were all quiet. 236 was starting to come out of her sedation, but was just standing silently next to me. We touched sides to try and stabilize one another, and maybe to give eachother comfort that we were going to die together. The horse tied at the end, near the door of the trailer was young, maybe 8 months old and she was awfully skinny. As much as I tried to avoid the thought, I wasn't sure how they were going to get anything to eat off of that filly at all, there was just nothing to her. Next to her was a buckskin gelding, he was 12. We had spoken a few times when I had first arrived, but we weren't overly familiar. He looked okay, he was a "hard keeper" that his owner didn't want to feed through the winter.

Our drive was a long one, with many stops along the way. From time to time the man and woman would come back to the trailer and talk to us, offer us water. The filly and the buckskin drank a lot, 236 took some, and I had decided not to give them the benefit of a juicy meal later and declined.

I was thirsty, but they can go to hell.

It was dark by the time we got where we were going. They unloaded us and put us each in a separate stall, though we were all in earshot of one another. It was too dark to see and that made me nervous, but I could hear other horses calling. There is fresh water and hay in a pile in the corner.

I guess death will meet us in the morning.

236's Journal

The monsters took us by force. They loaded us onto the trailer, there were only 4 of us. I got some good licks in before they drugged me, but they weren't enough to keep us from death's door. They gave us water throughout our trip and now we have been unloaded into smaller pens, separate from each other. I paced for a while and then softly called for Grandma, afraid that she was already dead. I heard her sweet voice call back through the darkness, "I am here." She was close by, maybe a few feet away. I tested the panels of my pen, but they were strong and solid.

At least we were together, for now.

Sherry's Journal

They are here, they are safe. We headed back out to the kill pens to pick up the horses this morning. I really thought that big mare was going to kill Joe. She was biting and lunging at us from over the fence while we tried to get Lady. Once we got her safe into a stall and sedated Lady lashed out and kicked Joe. His ear is ringing and he's got some bruising, but he'll be okay.

It was exhausting. We got home late tonight and were able to get everyone settled into quarantine without an issue. I'll have to go out in a little while and check on Lady though, she didn't drink any water on the way out.

July 2

236 is in a stall a few feet away, we are in a barn, and while I can't see most of the other horses, just the ones in here- I count about 40 different voices. Forty doomed souls. Those people are around constantly, I found out that the woman's name is Sherry, and the man who was always with her at the other pens, is Joe.

That vet was with them again today, and a farrier. I was ready for a fight, but a stall is not the best place to run away and they caught me pretty quick. The vet came in and gave me a shot and I started to drift away...

Duke and I had come from the same ranch, our momma's were friends. When we went to live with owner we were just walked over. They lived just down the road from where we were born. We would see our mommas from time to time, when the neighbor would help with brandings. Duke was a good horse and a good friend. We worked a lot of years together. It seems like forever ago now, but it must have been only a little over a month ago that I lost him to colic. I remember his face so clearly, always chipper, always so alive. 236 reminds me a little of Duke, just a naturally kind soul.

When I came out of the fog, I noticed that my feet had been trimmed- and my stifle doesn't hurt so much now. I was back in the stall, and my heart ached for my home, which I guess is not my home any longer. I am at a 4th different place in 2 months.

I don't have a home.

They tried to catch 236, but she was lunging at them and baring her teeth. They thought better of it and backed off. The woman is bold though, I will give her credit for that. She only left for a little while before coming back with a bag of apples. I love apples. She offered me one, "Come on, Lady." I checked her hands to make sure there wasn't a halter in it, and then carefully reached out and took one. God, it was delicious.

Then she approached 236, who again lunged and bared her teeth. This woman, Sherry, just sat down a few feet away from 236's pen and rolled an apple into the pen which caused 236 to jump a little. She kept saying, "Come on honey, it's alright." But she didn't approach again, she just sat there on the floor quietly in front of 236's pen. After about an hour, I nickered softly to 236 that the apples are good. "What's the worst that's going to happen? We are going to die here anyway."

236 looked at me and huffed, but she took the apple off the ground. Sherry stood up, "Good girl, Honey." and left. At first I thought she was saying honey, like you do to children. I would call my daughter honey sometimes, but I think she gave 236 a name. Why give a name to something you intend to destroy?

236's Journal

I saw what they did to Grandma, there was NO WAY! I gave all the show that I had in me. I was terrified, but I wasn't going to let them know that. I don't like being mean, but if I'm dying today then so are you, freaking monsters.

The female came back a little while later, with a bag of something. She offered one to Grandma and called her "Lady." I realized that I didn't even know her name, but I like Grandma better than Lady, so I'm going to stick with that. Grandma took the round thing warily, carefully. But for a moment, she looked like she was in heaven.

The monster came over to my pen, but I made like I would kill her if she tried so she backed up and sat down, out of reach. She rolled one of the round things towards me. Yeah right! Like I am going to trust a monster, I was for sure that it was a trap. After a while Grandma, in her lovingly condescending voice said, "Take it, they're good. What is the worst that could happen? We are going to die anyway."

I looked at Grandma, a little surprised, and huffed. We are standing at death's door and she's making jokes. But I tried the ball, apparently called an apple. It was like nothing I have ever had before. When I bit into it there were so many things going on in my mouth.

It was crunchy, sweet, but somehow soft and full of sticky sweet water, like a hope that I would never live to see- all wrapped up in a ball in my mouth. As soon as I ate it, the monster got up. I tensed, but she just said "good girl, honey," and then she left. Grandma said that they replaced my number with a name.
"Honey"

I have never had a name.

Sherry's Journal

I think Lady will come around just fine with some time. She is nervous and timid, but she seems willing to interact, especially when there are treats involved. The other two light horses appear to be pretty fond of people in general. That big girl though, she's the type of mare that hits me right in the heartstrings. I have named her Honey, I'm hoping that a new name may just be the beginning of a new life for this poor scared mare. I know that she is dangerous right now, but it's all out of fear, she is not actively aggressive, she tries to defend herself and her friend, Lady.

I think there is something phenomenally special about this mare. I hope that she comes around, that her damage does not run too deep. The PMU horses are always the hardest. It makes me emotional. I cry often when I see horses like her, the damage that humanity has done to these typically soft and kind hearted creatures. I wish I could explain to her, that she is okay now. But that is something we have to show, not just say.

July 3

The skinny girl that was on the trailer with us is down the way a little bit. They have been giving her grain and Sherry spends time early every morning, petting her and talking to her. They call her Grace. The filly seems to like her name and she seems to be coming around to Sherry.

Sherry and the man, Joe, both come around and talk to me. I turn my butt and feign like I'm going to kick; how do they expect me to make friends with the animals that are going to eat me. Sherry is an odd one though, she just laughs a little and moves on. Like she knows I'm faking. All they want is to lead to my death quietly, and I'm not going to give them that. If they have no consideration for the life of the horse, why should I give them any consideration at all?

Today I thought about Mac. I wonder if he had to wait in anticipation of death, the same way that we are having to wait. It's torturous. I know there is food and water and it's clean here, but I also know that death beckons to us, that we have been marked for slaughter. To be squeezed into a little chute and have our throats slit. That's how they did it at the farm, to the pigs. I saw it once, the fear, the confusion, and then the gurgling sound and slightly coppery smell of blood that filled the air- the smell of death. This place doesn't smell like death, but that's what they had said at the pens- we are slaughter bound.

236, I mean Honey, does not appear to be going without a fight. She's not giving an inch. I don't blame her. I thought I had a rough go of things before I ended up at that first auction house, but my life has been nothing compared to hers. I wouldn't have any faith in people either. I don't trust them, but I think Honey is genuinely terrified of them. She's a good soul, she is kind and sweet and is a good friend. I am glad that I have her here, that I am not going to die alone.

236's Journal

The monster's call me Honey. It's odd to have a name, but I suppose it's just a different inventory classification. They prefer to destroy things with names. They want to make it personal, get to know you, earn your trust and then kill you. I don't understand how any animal could be so genuinely cruel. Horses are honest folk, everything we do, everything we feel, everything we present is honest. The monsters don't offer honesty in any way. They are beasts without souls.

I had a flashback again. I was back at the PMU facility. Exhausted, delusional from sleep deprivation. I started to fall asleep while I was standing and my knees kept hitting the bar of my stall, the rope they kept around my belly would cut in and force me to stand even when I didn't think I could. They call it a stall, but the space is just big enough to squeeze a horse into, there is literally contact on every side. Don't they know that we have to lay down to get our REM sleep? We literally go crazy from not sleeping. It was a horrible life. The mares that weren't strong enough were shipped off, I suppose I know where they went now.

From the factory to the table.

I still have my mind, at least most of the time, except for the flashbacks. But I'll be damned if I ever trust even one of the monsters. They are nothing but ushers of pain and death.

July 5

Sherry and Joe always seem to be here. I wonder if they are the ones who kill us or if they hire on a hand that does that for them. At the farm, they hired someone who would come and "take care of the pigs." But they slaughtered the birds themselves. The anticipation here is sickening. Sherry keeps trying to coax us closer, trying to touch us and while the little filly has given in, Honey and I are standing our ground.

I have seen kindness turn to viciousness too many times in my life. I fight not only for myself but for Mac and vainly for so many others that have been forced down this devastating road. Today Sherry came through and told Honey, "It's okay big girl we're here to take care of you."
I assume they do their own killing, and that like the pigs we will look death in the face before it takes us.

There was yet another person here with Sherry and Joe this evening, a little before feeding time. They were standing in front of my and Honey's pens. There was some discussion about us, they kept saying our names, but I can only understand some of their language. Most of what I understand from people comes from their body language. They often times don't realize how "loud" they are when they move and I have come to the conclusion that they really have no idea how to talk- they just make noise and move around a lot.

Anyway, what I did catch of the conversation is that Sherry was suggesting that Honey and I were a bonded pair. I am honestly surprised that they even recognize that fact given that Sherry and Joe are a bonded pair and they are oblivious to their own situation. They went on to talk about something called "rehabilitation", which seems like an awfully big term for such an archaic creature. Maybe it's a food term and these people have enough compassion to let us die together. I have no idea. They continued on that we would be in "quarantine" for another week, to make sure none of us came up sick. Well of course that makes sense, why would you want a horse half dead when you kill it.

The woman that I don't know approached my pen, after she was done talking with Sherry. I got into the furthest corner of my pen and avoided eye contact. This person moved with more intent, more confidence, more power through her body. She came to the edge of the pen and Honey tried to reach out and bite her, but the woman was out of reach. She didn't even flinch when Honey lunged, she knew exactly where her body was in relation to her environment. She started slowly towards the corner I was in and I bolted to the other corner. Please just go away, please just go away. I don't want to die today, please just go away. I had one ear on her to make sure I knew where she was, but I wasn't going to look at her. I couldn't bring myself to look at her.

She finally, after what seemed like hours (but was probably ten minutes), headed back to Sherry. She wrote something down in a notebook that she was carrying and said that I was still shut down and that I seemed terrified. Well I'm so glad that you are competent enough to figure out the obvious! They continued to discuss me and my "program." Honestly, do you lack so much compassion, that you are comfortable discussing what kind of meals I will become, right in front of me. Can't you at least go somewhere else?

I know, why don't we round up a bunch of humans and sell you off? We'll move you around and then tell you we are going to eat you. We'll pull you away from your family and friends and then you'll have to wait to meet death, the whole time knowing that you have been determined to die for absolutely no reason other than you aren't useful to us anymore!! You still wouldn't understand, it still wouldn't be the same. For the simple fact that we don't use you up first, we don't beat you, we don't work you into the ground, and rely on your instincts or your strength. You have no idea the damage you humans do, but you seem awfully content to do it.

The bold woman went to Honey's pen next, that did not go as well.

236's Journal

I hate the monsters. I can't forgive them for the life they made me lead, for my babies that I know they destroyed. For my mother, who was at the same factory. I watched her collapse in her stall while the rope ate into her belly and hind end, heavily pregnant, her knees shaking while she tried to get back up and simply couldn't. They beat her across the back and across the neck to convince her it was worth her while to stand back up. I knew from the look in her eyes that it was over...she was done. The spirit had all but left her, she was dying, her mind and her body had finally given up. I was devastated, but at the same time I was happy for her that she would not have to suffer in this place any longer. They unhooked her from everything and tried to force her into the aisle of the barn. All of the other horses were silent, our factory had become a tomb. We knew. She was able to right herself for but a moment before she collapsed in the alley and aborted her foal, 2 more beautiful souls lost for no reason.

Can't the monsters get what they need without killing us for our urine?! They put the baby in a trash bag. They took my mother out by dragging her through the barn with a tractor. An unspoken threat of compliance or death.

When I came out of my flashback, there were two people in our barn and I panicked because one of them was standing by Grandma's stall. I was afraid they were going to beat her like they did with my mother so I immediately lunged at the monster by Grandma's pen. I tried to bite her a few times, but she was just out of reach. I got nervous and started freaking out a little bit. The monster named Sherry was there and tried to talk me down, but I'm not having any of this!

The monster by Grandma's pen took caution and walked away, spoke to the Sherry monster for a moment and then made the foolish mistake of coming at me. Grandma said it looked like the monster was going to pet my face, but I am convinced that she was going to hit me for trying to bite her. So I defended myself, and I can move pretty fast for a big girl. I launched myself at her to bite her hand, but she moved at the last minute and I just ended up barely hitting her in the side of the face with my nose. I assume that she had planned for that because as my head slammed into her I felt her run her hand down my neck, softly- like a subtle threat that she was more than willing to slit my throat... I backed away quickly to the other end of my little pen. Don't touch me! Don't fucking touch me, you disgusting heartless beasts!!

Sherry's Journal

Taylor came to quarantine today to evaluate Lady and Honey. The other two horses seem okay and can be worked with by one of the volunteers, but Lady and Honey are going to need Taylor's attention if we are to have any hope of rehabilitating them. I really hope we can help them to be more comfortable with us and with their lives here. Taylor thinks that Lady will be okay with some time and patience, but she wasn't sure about Honey. Her damage runs very deep. For now Taylor will be the only one allowed to work with her other than Joe and myself. Taylor asked me what made me decide to get another crazy one, and all I could say was that she needed us. Isn't that enough?

Chapter 5: Transition

There are so many processes in the rescue of horses, there is so much hope that is sometimes not attained. Long before they are trusting, rescuers try to give the horse every opportunity. The gentle and willing animal is treated with the same respect and love as the horse that is aggressive and scared.

Rescuers and trainers who seek to help these horses often put their lives and safety at risk on behalf of these animals who do not understand that we are not the people of their past. We understand that reactivity, fear and trauma are part of what we work with. We also know that there is no greater moment than when a horse who has been fearful, avoiding, aggressive or otherwise behaviorally inhibited, shows that inch of trust. To see the horse that has been tense for days, weeks, months, years, finally be able to relax in an environment, often results in tearful responses from us, as the tenders of these beautiful creatures.

We take each day, with each individual horse, knowing that we cannot undo the damage of the past. It is our communal hope, that perhaps we can allow the scars to heal and in bandaging the wounds of the psyche, allow a horse to find some level of peace in their future.

July 7

Joe came through with Sherry. They had halters in their hands. They tried to coax me with an apple, but there was no way I was coming up and just giving in to my death. I thought I would be more composed when this moment came, but I was terrified; I am not ready to die.

My pen was not particularly large. There is enough room for me to move about, lie down, and roll but that's about it. We were at it for about half an hour. By the end we were all tired and frustrated. I was exhausted, sweaty, shaking from being anxious and afraid. Eventually though, they caught me. They brought me out of my pen and tied me to Honey's pen.

Honey came over and nuzzled me for a few minutes. The people stood back for a while and just gave us space and time with one another. We groomed and spoke softly to each other. For a horrible species, I appreciated the kindness of letting me say goodbye to my friend.

Sherry came up after a while and untied my lead. I hung my head, nickered goodbye to my dear Honey and followed Sherry, down the aisle, heading out of the barn. While I was not ready to die, I was resigned to it, and as we walked I began to drift back in my mind, away from this place. I was on my farm again. I didn't notice when we stopped just outside of the barn, though in my daze I could hear Honey calling...crying.

I was startled out of my dreaming by a nuzzle on my butt. I jumped and was ready to kick out at whatever had touched me, when in a moment I realized it was Honey. They had caught her, we were going to die together. As sad as I was that Honey would lose her beautiful and precious life, I was glad that neither of us would have to venture this hell alone.

They walked us up and down the aisle of the barn together for about an hour. I could see the daylight outside of the barn and longed to feel it on my tired soul again, but we weren't taken outside. As we paced up and down together I saw other horses outside, in pasture full of lush grass. Some of them were laying down, some were standing around looking contented. There were young ones who were playing in a far field- I didn't see any mares with them, just babies ranging from about two months old to about a year old. This is not what I had pictured our transition to hell would be like.

Joe was walking Honey. From time to time he would reach out and try to touch her side and she would tense hard and move away from the contact. He would bring his hand back to himself gently and talk to her softly, "It's okay Honey, it's alright big girl."

They put us back in our stalls after a while, but they left our halters on. It was an unsettling encounter.

236's Journal

They ran Grandma to exhaustion in her pen and when there was finally nothing left for her to give, they put a halter on her and brought her out. They tied her to my pen for a while. I was so glad for the contact. I had missed my friend- even though we were only a few feet away. She calms me and I feel like while I am her protector, she is my balance. I pinned my ears at the monsters, but I didn't try to bite or rush any of them, because I coveted this time with my friend.

We spoke and touched and forgot about our fate for a while. It was an intimate but solemn goodbye. The female monster approached and again I pinned my ears, but did not rush her, so as not to hurt Grandma in the process. The monster untied Grandma and began to take her away. Grandma looked like she had given up, I was so sad and angry. I called for her desperately, I didn't want her to have to go alone. I didn't want her to die...I didn't want to BE alone with the monsters. I began to pace nervously. The male monster approached my pen carefully, with a halter. I was pacing and calling and as he approached and held the halter out for me to sniff at I jammed my head down into it. I'll take the risk, just take me back to my friend!!

And to my surprise, he did.

We walked to the edge of the aisle and Grandma was there, just around the corner. I reached out and nuzzled her as softly as I could, she startled a little bit and I thought she was going to kick my head off, but then she realized it was me and relaxed. The monsters walked us up and down the aisle for a while. Every now and then the man would try to hit me for no reason and I would tense and step away, ready for the blow; he pulled his hand back every time and would babble something at me that I ignored. I have no time to present myself complacent to these ushers of death. But I was glad to be with Grandma, that was all that I cared about.

Grandma was looking around at what was going on outside, I was mostly looking at Grandma. At one point she told me to look, and out in a far pasture full of green were babies playing and running. For a split second I looked for my children, I may have even called- I don't remember. My heart was full and more broken all in an instant as I remembered my children, that they are not here. After a while of walking back and forth they put us back in our pens, but they didn't take off our halters. I took that as a sign that death was nearing.

Sherry's Journal
We tried a new tactic with Lady and Honey today. Joe and I were both very nervous, but the stalls needed to be cleaned and it wouldn't hurt the girls to get out of them for a little while and walk. We used Lady to bait Honey in order to catch her, hoping that she would be more willing to catch by taking her friend out of sight. It worked. No one got hurt, the girls got to walk and the stalls got cleaned. At least now we seem to have a baby step for the girls. They are a phenomenally bonded pair. Surprisingly, Honey is a scared but sweet and obedient horse once she is caught. She doesn't seem to spook at much in her environment, just at the touch of people. I wish there was some way to explain to her that she is safe here, but only time will tell her that.

July 9

Each day they take us out and walk us down the aisle. First they take me out and around the corner, so they can catch Honey. We walk for about an hour each day, just up and down the aisle. And then they take the filly out for a while, and lastly the Buckskin gelding. I assume that we taste better if we are exercised and have good muscle tone. I have no idea. There is no other explanation for their weird behavior.

The gelding seems to be fond of people, he is gracious, respectful and likes the attention. I see him reach for them, begging them touch him when they come through. The filly is similarly so, eager for the interaction, and a glutton for scratches. The filly is putting on weight well, she is starting to look healthier, but I fear for her and can't bring myself to tell her that they are just fattening her up to slaughter her. Although I don't know when that time will come, even Sherry and Joe said it when we were at the previous pens that we are "slaughter bound."

July 12

There were a lot of people here. Sherry was leading a group of them around, she called them "volunteers." She brought them through our barn and called it "quarantine." She had called it that before, but today she spent a lot of time in our barn. Taking her group and standing in front of each pen, talking about the individual horses. I listened intently, I am learning more of their language, although they completely suck at learning ours.

She started with the filly.
"This is Grace. She is a nurse mare foal that we acquired from a kill pen. She was severely underweight and unhandled. She is learning to lead and be groomed and most of our focus is on getting her up to weight and socialized so that she can find a forever family of her own.

For those who don't know what a nurse mare foal is: On large ranches and breeding farms there are mares who are bred specifically to nurse foals that are not theirs. If a 'valuable' mare dies during labor or before a foal is weaned, then the 'more valuable' foal is placed with the nurse mare and the native foal is discarded as trash. Thousands of mares are bred every year for this purpose alone- to have their babies thrown away so they can nurse and raise foals which are considered more deserving of a chance to live. The foals which are discarded are anywhere from newborns to about 8 months old depending on the situation. Some of the foals are 'culled' which is just a different word for killed. Occasionally they are sold, but a good portion of them, like our little Grace here are discarded to kill pens and shipped to slaughter. We intercepted Grace because of donations made on her behalf and she will be rehabilitated with us until she is placed with a suitable family."

There was conversation back and forth between the group and everyone gathered around to give the filly, I now know as "Grace," some loving. They then moved on to the buckskin gelding. I continued to listen and watch this odd menagerie.

"This is Sam. He is an 12 year old quarter horse gelding. He was originally purchased as a trail horse, but he requires a little more feed than some of our other horses to keep a good weight on. His family sent him to auction because they didn't want to have to feed a 'hard keeper' through the winter. He was purchased by a kill pen and was destined for slaughter. He is super friendly and broke to ride and we are hoping that after his time here in quarantine we can tune him up and find a family that will value this very sweet boy."

Again the pack of people gathered around the pen and scratched, pet and engaged the willing horse. Next was Honey and I was eager to listen to what Sherry had to say about my sweet friend.

"This is Honey. She is a PMU mare. She is about 15 years old. PMU stands for Premarin, which is a type of hormone drug that is given to women to regulate their estrogen levels. Premarin stands for Pregnant Mare Urine, it's an acronym. These mares are kept pregnant, in very small standing stalls all day and all night, they have catheters inserted into their vaginas to harvest urine 24/7 and strapping around their flanks which is affixed to the ceiling or to beams to keep their back ends up, and non-mobile. They are unable to lay down. While it is common knowledge that horses can nap standing up, the only way for a horse to get a REM sleep is to lie down. These mares are deprived of that for months on end, for years.

When it is time for them to foal, their babies are taken from them, and much like nurse mare foals are killed, sold, or sent to slaughter. Often their babies are sent to Japan, and killed on site so that the foals may be served raw. They are considered nothing more than a byproduct of an industry. The mares are then rebred to keep them pregnant and the cycle of hell continues for these horses. When a mare can no longer breed or her estrogen levels deplete, they send them to slaughter- no longer useful enough to live. A large portion of PMU mares cannot be rehabilitated due to the effects of sleep deprivation, fatigue, abuse and neglect they become unstable, unpredictable and they are turned into sanctuary horses which will not be adopted out.

Honey here is very defensive aggressive, and understandably so, given what she has been through. We are hoping that with time and patience, she can be rehabilitated, but if not she will remain here with us as a sanctuary horse and live out the rest of her days free, safe and as comfortable as we can make her. She is deeply bonded to our next horse, Lady."

The group attempted to gather around Honey, but you could see that Honey was not comfortable with the approach. Honey began to tense and looked like she was going to panic when Sherry stopped them saying that my large friend needed more time and that a group of people would be just too much for her to handle. Sherry earned an inch of respect from me today.

I was overwhelmed by Honey's story and was even more honored that she considered me a friend. I was suddenly overtaken with a realization, I didn't know why I was here, why I was cast aside by my owners. Today I was going to learn my own story. Sherry made her way over to me and it seemed to take forever. I was watching, waiting for her to begin.

"This is Lady. She is a 22 year old Quarter Horse. She was a former ranch horse who we suspect was abused. She is very smart and very sweet, but she is head shy, timid and untrusting. She is broke to ride, but is difficult to catch because of her trust issues. She was sold at auction simply because of her age, she is sound and kind, but it will take a very special person to adopt her. This mare is very sweet, but she will require patience and someone who is willing to work with her on her terms. She is our wonderful wary mare."

I was stunned! That's it? I was sent to my death simply because I aged? We all age! That angry old cuss that I hauled around for so many years was old! No one was shipping him off to hell! My mind was spinning, my heart was broken. I was...AM still a good and useful partner, but the natural process of time has rendered me months of pain, horror, and ultimately a harsh fate at the hands of people. I don't even know what to say. I looked over at Honey, she was crying; she wasn't making a sound but I could see the tears streaming down her face.

236's Journal

I am in shock. I just don't know what else to say. They brought a big group of monsters through today. They went to each of our four pens and told the other monsters our stories. It was different, hearing my story out loud, listening to the fate of my children, my fate. It made me so horribly sad and angry. THEY KNOW!
*They know what happens to us. They know what we go through, what our babies go through. They **know**? And yet they do nothing, they let us go crazy, they let us die, they let us have baby after baby and watch that precious life get thrown away like they are nothing, like we are nothing. There are THOUSANDS of us! Anger seethed in me like never before and the emotions were just too much to handle. I tried desperately to not show that they had gotten to me, but when they headed over towards Grandma, I broke.*

Sherry's Journal
Today was the first day of orientation. We have ten new volunteers to introduce. I love when people have a passion to help and we always need the help. We started in quarantine as usual. We give the histories

of the horses that are in QT and while I try not to let my emotions interfere, it is always very personal for me. The fact that we have a nurse mare foal and a PMU horse in there right now, I think was very eye opening for some of our volunteers. The hardships that these horses face seems to be more real when they are standing in front of you.

We spent about 4 hours going over the whole ranch. Over the next 3 days we will go through handling horses and all of the other aspects of what our volunteers will have the opportunity to do here with us. I always hope to instill not only a passion to help but a drive to make a difference, to give the horses a voice.

July 13

I had trouble sleeping last night, my mind was spinning, my heart was wrecked. My life, my work everything was a waste. It was all for nothing. What hope do we have as horses when at a whim, humans just discard us as trash, for no reason whatsoever. We are not things, we are beings. I think Honey is right to call them monsters.

July 14

They fed us earlier than usual this morning. After breakfast, Joe came and took the little filly, Grace. He just haltered her and took her away, out of the barn. I knew it was time. They had made a spectacle of us yesterday, breaking us down to nothing, even Honey was quiet. Now we were being taken one by one. I knew today was the day we were erased from the memory of the world.

Joe came back and haltered Sam, leading him away into the newly rising sun. I looked over at Honey, I think she died a little bit inside since the other day. My dear friend and constant companion seemed, at this point, to welcome death. It was a long time before Joe returned, and Sherry was with him. Sherry headed towards me, I assume to go through the same routine that we always go through before catching Honey. But Joe called quietly to Sherry before she could begin to chase me around my pen. Sherry stopped and looked over, so did I.

Joe was standing in Honey's stall, with her haltered and on a lead line, her head was so low to the ground that I thought she might tip over. It broke my heart to see this strong soul so utterly devastated. They unhooked the lead rope from Honey's halter and stepped out of the stall. Honey never even twitched an ear. Sherry was on the phone with someone, probably the vet, saying that there was something wrong with Honey and that he needed to get to the ranch as soon as possible.

They left us in our pens in the barn. I assumed that they didn't want to eat meat from a sick animal which is why we are alive right now. I tried not to think about Grace or Sam, I had to push their faces to the darkest corners of my mind. Right now, my friend needed me. "Honey." I nickered ever so softly. "Honey, sweetie, are you okay?" The lift of her head was barely perceptible.

"Grandma...I," she choked up, "I just don't think I can."

I knew what she meant, there was nothing left to give, nothing left to hope for, nothing left to feel, just nothing left. As I was about to respond Sherry came in with the vet. Honey never even flinched when the vet gave her the shot that makes you sleepy drunk. He checked her over, took blood, took some of her poop from the corner, but in the end he told Sherry that there didn't seem to be any physical ailment, Honey was depressed. Apparently we are going to be breathing for a few more days while he checks the bloodwork, and all it cost was Honey's heart.

236's Journal

Honestly I don't even know what to write, I am broken, and I welcome death. The monsters came, they poked prodded and did things. We didn't die today...I wish we had.

Sherry's Journal
Joe and I stuck to our plan with the girls today, so that we could get poor scared Honey out of QT and into a pasture. Hopefully, she and Lady could settle in and get some time to just be horses for a while. We got Grace and Sam out to their designated pastures without a hitch and headed back for the girls. Catching Honey is always tricky but we have developed a system that is safe and seems to work. I hate sedating horses if we can avoid it. Before I could even get to Lady's stall I heard Joe, whispering, but calling as though he were trying to quietly yell. It was an unnatural noise for him to make and before I could snap at him I looked over my shoulder. He was standing there, attached to Honey. The mare looked lethargic so we called the vet. Honey didn't bat an eye while he gave her a mild sedative to keep everyone safe, took blood, and did a full physical. He thinks that she is just depressed, but they will stay in QT for now, until we get results back from her workup.

July 17

I slept without dreaming last night. I was so exhausted, emotionally drained, and I felt guilty. I thought my past was hard, but Honey has never caught a break, not once. She was mentally abused, physically abused, and then cast aside. I remembered when she first showed up at the kill pens, she had asked me if we were allowed to lay down. It seemed like such an odd question, but I get it now.

God what a horrible life for a sentient soul. My heart just absolutely broke for my friend. As I looked at her, forlorn, drained of any hope or strength that she had, I just whispered, "I'm so very sorry." There was no response from Honey, and I felt stupid for saying something so inadequate.

Sherry and Joe came in sometime in the afternoon. Joe went cautiously towards Honey, who still had not responded to much of anything, including food. He hooked up, shrugged his shoulders and spoke softly to her. He didn't try to touch her, just spoke to her. Apparently she was healthy enough to die today.

Sherry came and chased me around, but I caught sight of Honey in my periphery and gave up; allowing myself to be caught rather quickly. "Come on old girl," Sherry whispered to me, "your friend needs you." I was surprised at the comment. It was laden with genuine concern. This particular human seems to, at least to some point, care.

Sherry lead me a little ahead. I didn't know if Honey was going to move, but my dear giant friend can move rather lithe when it suits.

She moved quietly, slowly and resigned. Sherry slowed her pace so that Honey and I could walk close to one another, and we did. My right side was pressed up against her left side as we strode together, both prepared to die.

They brought us to a paddock, that had tall grass in it, it was about the size of a large arena. There were horses in pastures and paddocks on all sides of it. They walked us through the gate and took off the lead ropes, but left our halters on. It was just Honey and I, standing alone in a field of grass. Suddenly, Honey spoke.

"Grandma." Honey whispered to me. "Grandma, what is this?" She was staring at the ground.

"What?" I was completely taken aback. She couldn't possibly not know what *grass* is. "What is what?" I cocked my head slightly, somewhat dumbfounded by the situation I had now found myself in.

"What is *this?*" She repeated, pawing at the ground. Slowly she lifted her head with a look of genuine concern. She portrayed an innocence that I had never seen in my friend, not since the first time we met; but even that was more of excited naivete. This was unadulterated innocence, concern, curiosity.

My heart broke a little more for this tender soul. "Sweetheart, that's grass. It's good for naps and snacks." In an instant that mare went down with a thud, she groaned and stretched out as far as her body would allow, rolled for a moment and then just laid there on her side. After a while, I walked around the head end of her because she hadn't gotten back up. She was sound asleep. Hard, deep sleep in the grass and the sunshine. My heart was full of joy and sorrow all intermingled for this sweet mare. For a little while, we forgot about the struggles that life held. I stood sentry over her while she slept. We were the only two horses in our little paddock, but I stood watch over her nonetheless, warming my bones and just purely enjoying the warm sunshine and the tantalizing sweet smell of wet grass.

236's Journal

The morning was all a blur, a deep depressing haze of determined death. We were led and turned out into a small pasture area and I experienced grass for the first time. It was just me and Grandma in our space, and it was a good sized space. I laid down in the grass and drifted away into a deep sleep.

I woke up in a panic, for a moment I forgot where I was. I felt the wet grass on my face, and I thought I had fallen down from exhaustion- in my stocks, at the PMU factory. I struggled to get up but I kept slipping. I thought I was slipping in my own blood and I screamed, until Grandma pawed me in the face. She nuzzled me for a moment, her soft and tender voice chimed, "Easy, dear one. You were dreaming, you're okay. Easy." I calmed down immediately and lie there for a while, letting the sunshine beat down on my face. My body ached, but in a good way, I don't think I have ever slept for so long.

For a few moments the world was transformed into something beautiful, but it didn't take long for our current situation and the past few weeks to come rushing back to me in a flood. Despair regained it's

hold on my heart, but at least I had Grandma. We had eachother for
now.

Sherry's Journal
Sometimes I wonder if horses understand so much more than we give them credit for. I know that at least some do. I believe that Lady is a horse like that. While she can be hard to catch she "gets it.' I don't know how to explain it better than that. Buck, our old mustang is that way. It's like some of them understand when we talk to them, they are intuitively responsive, different, extra special. I am always so appreciative when these horses enter my life and allow me to be a part of theirs. It's like God sends an angel to help both the other horses, and the humans that are trying to make a difference. We got the girls moved out to pasture today. Turned them loose, walked away a little ways and stopped to watch how our big depressed girl would react. It was odd, as though she had never been in grass before, she just stood there with her head down for a while, a little tense. Then she pawed at it and went down like a ton of bricks. I tried not to cry, but I couldn't help myself. It was a beautiful moment.

Chapter 6: Rehabilitation Takes Time

Rehabilitating horses that have a past can take days to years, depending on the damage, and depending on the horse. It takes a lot of patience, it takes a lot of humor and it takes a lot of heart. For some, this struggle begins with the simple obstacle of touch and trust. Rehabilitation is not just about retraining a horse. It is about overcoming ideas and behaviors that have already been ingrained and trained into the horse regarding who we are, as people, as a species. We have to attribute reactivity, have patience in allowing horses to overcome that reactivity. Then attempt to teach them to unlearn things, before we can effectively teach them to learn anything new. Even if we can succeed in overcoming these hurdles with horses, we are not working with a new animal, we are still working with a horse that has a past, has struggles to overcome at every turn in our effort to give them a future.

July 19

The last two days have been a lot. They have been amazing and quiet, but Honey and I both had an overwhelming influx of emotions and things to process. Our bond just keeps getting stronger and we are becoming very good friends.

There was a woman that came around today and stood at our gate. Honey and I both headed for the far side of the field. The woman waited until we were situated and then she came in. She didn't have halters, leads, or anything with her, but she looked familiar and I was trying to place where I had seen her before. She came towards us slowly, but with a self assurance that I had not previously seen in most people. Maybe she was hungry? She did look kind of thin.

It hit me, the woman from quarantine- the confident one that approached our pens but didn't try to mess with us, she had been with Sherry. She stood in the middle of our field, just stood there. "Hey girls, I'm Taylor and I'm going to be working with you guys." She began to walk closer to us, but stopped about fifteen feet away, when she saw we were getting nervous with her presence. Honey started to arch and get ready to bolt and Taylor took a step back to give us just a little more space, just enough to keep us there. "See there," she spoke calmly but powerfully, "that's good. I know you guys have had a rough go of life and that trust is not something that you give easily. Just know that you're safe here, nothing here, nobody here, wants to hurt you." She took a few steps backwards while still facing us, and then turned to leave. Just as Honey and I began to relax, Taylor stopped and turned to face us again. "Oh, I almost forgot!" and she pulled something out of her pocket and placed it on the ground in the grass. I didn't see what it was- I was too busy watching *her*.

Honey and I approached the spot where she had been. Honey saw them first, huffed and hopped backwards a little bit. I looked down, and there were a couple of carrots. They looked good, they smelled okay, I reassured Honey and we each had one. I looked up and the Taylor woman was not five feet away from us at the gate, smiling.

236's Journal

There was a monster here, in our pen today. She was small but there was something powerful about her. She pinned us in a corner and stood in the middle of our field- taunting us, daring us to run. She looked as though she was ready to pounce at any moment. She is different than the other monsters, light on her feet, always ready to move. Her body language was relaxed, but I could tell that she had good reflexes and I wasn't about to test my limits with this one. She stayed for maybe fifteen or twenty minutes and then placed something on the ground just inside our pen. As we approached, I felt in my bones that it was a trap, and when we came across the orange stakes that she had left on the ground, I startled. Grandma investigated and picked one up and ate it! She urged me to take the other one, a "carrot" she calls them. They were as good as the apple in quarantine. When I looked up, the monster was there, baring her teeth at us. I don't like this monster, I don't like any of them, but I am especially afraid of this one.

I watched the monster carefully throughout the day, as she went into pastures, led horses away out of my sight, and then she would return them to their pens after about an hour. I didn't see her hit any of them, but they weren't in my sight for long. Most of the horses seemed willing to work with her, some even seemed eager, which disgusted me a little.

Sherry's Journal
I decided to have Taylor focus on Lady and Honey, at least for the time being. The volunteers and other hands can assist with the friendly and more responsive horses to keep them handled, groomed and worked. I think Lady and especially Honey would benefit from Taylor's special way with horses.

July 20th

There is a flurry of people here all the time, people fixing fences, working on gates, brushing horses, a farrier, people who feed, people who clean up poop out of the pens and fill waters, people everywhere all the time. I have never been in a place with so many humans, it makes me anxious. At least they all seem content to work around us, except a few.

Taylor was the one who brought us breakfast this morning around 5 o'clock, alfalfa and grain. She put our feed in the big feed bin that is in our pasture, and then she sat down on the edge of it. Honey and I stood in the corner and watched her, we waited her out. By 10 o'clock I was getting irritated, Taylor didn't even seem to notice, she was now sitting comfortably in the grass with her back against our feed bin, reading a book. I decided that instead of eating the food that she brought, I would just eat the grass, it's just as good in my opinion anyway. As I began to graze, Honey kept a wary eye on Taylor, by the heat of the day Honey was grazing too. Taylor stayed in our pen for about another hour and then got up and headed out, I kept grazing but watched her; Honey picked her head up and froze. That human is an odd one for sure.

236's Journal

The monster that was here yesterday, was back again today. She brought hay this morning and then sat and guarded the food, not allowing us to approach. Even once the day began to get hot, she stayed. She moved to the grass and sat down, leaning up against our feed bin, she had something that she was looking at, but just ignored us, forcing us to stand in the corner. Grandma eventually began to eat the grass. How dare this monster keep food from an old lady like Grandma, I was fuming. I wanted to do something, but I was afraid to do much of anything. I stood watch over Grandma for a while, but the monster never gave an inch. When my stomach began to rumble I too began to graze, but we stayed in our corner and I watched the monster carefully. After a while she got up and left. Grandma turned an ear and was paying closer attention than she let on, smart old girl. I, on the other hand made it very clear that I was aware of the beast and her movements. Vile creatures.

July 21

It was crazier than usual at the ranch today. There were people painting fencing and barns. About 20 horses were moved to the far side of the ranch, I could see some of them in big stalls with bedding all laid down and fluffy. The ones they call volunteers were pulling horses out left and right, brushing, grooming, cleaning everything and everyone up. There were braids in manes and tails, and baths. For a moment I felt a longing.

It's been a long time since I had a bath- that cool water washing over everything, all the dirt, grime and sweat from days of hard work being washed away. It always seemed to soothe the sore muscles and refresh the world around me. The old man used some super foamy stuff and a curry comb and it was like a massage that went right down to my soul. He was half hearted about it, but even still I enjoyed it completely.

There was an old horse in the pasture next to us that was being haltered by one of the volunteers. I asked him what was going on?

"Tomorrow is our Adopt An Angel event. All the horses that are available for adoption are placed out for people to come and meet, play with, ride, whatever. I am a sanctuary horse, I don't get adopted, but they like to put me with the babies that get nervous or need a buddy. I'm the ranch babysitter." And then he was off, walking happily and proudly to help a nervous baby. I will have to ask him more about this when he returns.

What is "adoption?" What is "sanctuary?" How do I get a bath? Adoption sounds a lot like auction, do the people that come to see the horses look at them and mess with them so the horses are easier to slaughter? It seems like the more question I ask, leave me with only more questions.

As I pondered all this information, I saw a couple people go to the pasture where the nurse mare foals were kept. They took three of them out and I panicked. I began to pace and call, God please no- not the babies! They are just babies! Take me, kill me! Please not the babies! I called and called and paced myself into a sweat. In my frantic effort, I slipped and banged my head hard against the fence post. One of the volunteers saw it and ran the other way, hollering for Sherry and Taylor. Great, just what I need.

236's Journal

There was a lot going on today, Grandma was talking to the gimpy horse in the pasture next to us. I don't know what was said but after a while Grandma started to freak out and call to the babies that were being led away. She slipped and busted her face open on the fence. She was bleeding pretty bad. I remembered what happened to my mother when she went down at the factory and I was afraid that I would lose Grandma. Two of the monsters came running to our paddock and I was in between them and Grandma.

I was not about to let them beat her, she was already hurt and scared. I pinned my ears and rushed the fence. When Grandma got too close, I ushered her away and wouldn't let them near her. I turned my butt and kicked out and kept myself between Grandma and the monsters as best I could. Grandma was having a hard time seeing and she was already sweaty and shaking.

The skinny monster managed to get us split up when we headed for the back fence, Grandma went the opposite way and I ended up in a corner. The skinny monster stayed in between me and Grandma and was trying to talk to me, I tried to get around her but she was quick and light just like I knew she would be. The Sherry monster got a halter on Grandma, took her out of the paddock and shut the gate. As the Sherry monster started to walk Grandma away the skinny monster, they call her "Taylor" let me past her, I slammed that gate as hard as I could. It gave a little and made a loud noise when I hit it, I hurt my chest, but the Sherry monster stopped. She said something to the Taylor monster who headed out of sight.

The Sherry monster brought Grandma back, but not in to the pasture. Barely close enough that I could touch her. When the Taylor monster came back the vet was with her. It all happened quickly. When I reached out to touch Grandma I felt a prick in my neck and started getting sleepy.

Sherry's Journal
Tomorrow is our Adopt An Angel event, which makes today one of our busiest days of the year. Creating signs for each of our 52 horses, arranging food, directing volunteers, organizing, printing forms, advertising, helping with cleaning up and maintenance. Today we spend getting ready and then we do home checks and reference checks for about 2 weeks. It's exhausting, but exciting. I love seeing the horses getting an opportunity for new lives and loving futures. It also gives us the next round of adoption fees that helps to save more horses, who are currently awaiting death.
We always hope things go smoothly, but there is nearly always a hitch. Lady panicked about something and banged herself up pretty good. The vet had to sedate Honey and Lady, then clean and stitch up Lady's face. We really didn't need another vet bill right now, but I had enough in savings so that I wouldn't have to take money out of the ranch funds, they are slim enough as it is.

July 22

They doped Honey, they doped me too, but not as much as they did
with her. I am worried for my friend, she needs me. They took me to
a different barn, not the one they call quarantine, and began to clean
up my face. I apparently was bleeding, the cloth they were using
turned the water a deep red. Taylor, Sherry, Joe and the vet were all
there. Taylor held my lead rope while the others were working on me,
checking me over, doing all kinds of things. Taylor mentioned that
she was impressed that I was tolerating the procedure and being
handled, so well. I thought, "what did you expect? I have done it all
my life. I'm a *good horse.*"

As they were working on my face Taylor began to pet my neck gently,
and then began to braid my mane, like the old man's wife use to. I
wandered in my mind for a moment and was back on the farm. My
owner's wife had just handed me an apple, I started chewing and
leaned in just a little, it was nice to feel a gentle touch. I came to,
realized and righted myself. Taylor just laughed a little and
whispered, "Oh don't worry old girl, no one saw you trust me for a
sec." I looked over at her and she was smiling, but she looked like she
was crying a little too. She saw that I was looking, "It's alright
momma, I'm just happy that you gave me the benefit of the doubt
for a moment. That's all." She seemed...sincere.

After they cleaned me up, they gave me another shot which made my
face hurt less. Taylor took me back out and tied me to a tie rack, it
was hot out and I thought that maybe I had given her too much
credit; until I felt the cool water on my legs. She was giving me a bath.

236's Journal

I was back. I could feel the pressure of the stall on my sides and the beautiful child in my belly was moving around wildly. I was raw around my belly and my hips from the strap that was cutting in. My legs were swollen and my feet hurt so badly that I had to continuously shift my weight, but there was only so much I could shift. I was stressed and I was young, only 2 years old. It wasn't time for her to come yet, we still had months to go; but I felt my body cramping and start to give. I screamed and I wasn't sure exactly what was going on. My mind, my body was so very tired. I felt the pain in my hind end and the splash of my water breaking. Then she was gone.

I nearly collapsed, I would have collapsed, but I couldn't, the strap was holding my hind end and my head was tied. There was nowhere to go. I turned my head a little bit to try and see, I called to her, and then I nickered. Wake up baby. God, she was so small. The monster heard the commotion and came through, he kicked her a little with his foot. I didn't want him to touch her. I tried to kick him, but there was a short wall between he and I. Another monster came in and they put her in a wheelbarrow and took her away. They unhooked me and took me out of the stall. I was pregnant again within a few days, and put back in my stall.

When I came out of the sedation Grandma had been brought back to the pasture. She was clean and shiny and smelled funny, her face was swollen, but they had stitched her up and her mane was braided. She looked like a whole new horse, except for her face.

July 23

Taylor brought feed again this morning, early. She seemed chipper and in good spirits. "They will call me if they need me, until then I'm hanging with you ladies today." She said as she waved her phone around a little. As before, she dumped our feed in the bin and sat down on the edge of it. It was a good sized bin, a circle that I could probably stand comfortably in, like the cattle troughs they had at the farm.

After about a half an hour I headed towards the feed bin, on the opposite side of where Taylor was sitting. I carefully put my head down and began to eat. Honey was standing about 10 feet away, watching everything. I love that mare, she and I take good care of eachother. I told her to come eat. She approached slowly and her body was pressed up against mine. She stretched way out, like a foal. It was cute. She snagged a mouthful of hay and then took off back to her 10 ft safe place. We went through this back and forth until the hay was gone. Taylor never moved, really. She didn't try to pet, touch, catch or anything else, she sat there and pretty much ignored us until the hay was gone. She got down off the edge and sat on the grass for the rest of the day.

Today was the "Adopt An Angel event". There were people everywhere. Honey and I stayed in the middle of our little pasture and tried to avoid the masses as much as we could. It was like the auction house parade, but reversed. The horses were standing still and the people were on parade. It was awkward. Every now and then, someone would come by our pen and stop for a while, try to call us over, and then continue on to the other pens. People had apples and carrots and were handing them out to everyone. I could smell it in the air, the crisp sweetness, but I don't like strangers. Honey was shut down, it was all too much for her. She just ate a little bit and tried not to make eye contact with anyone or anything. Every now and then she would lay her head across my back and then go back to trying to hide her 17 hand bulk of a body behind my 15 hand self.

Things started to quiet down by dinner time. Taylor left. As soon as it looked like the mass of people had gone, Honey and I both went down hard, overstimulated. We both slept deeply, though neither of us tend to sleep for very long. When I woke up, Honey was standing quietly next to me, she was taking the first shift for the night.

236's Journal

There were so many monsters. They were everywhere, and sometimes would come to our pasture and try to get our attention. It was terrifying. Grandma stood with me in the middle of our pasture. She didn't seem to mind that I was hiding behind her, though she knows that if there were any danger, I would protect her. I just...there were so many of them.

July 26

Taylor has been in our pen every day, she seems okay in general. Sometimes she brings us apples or carrots. We are starting to settle in to this new place. Both Honey and I are still waiting for our death, but I suppose that this is an okay place to spend the days we have left. Honey and I talked for a long time last night about this Taylor girl, and I think we came to an agreement.

So when Taylor came this morning, I approached her. She smiled and greeted me kindly, she went to pet the side of my face and I reacted, deep down I'm still waiting for the blow. She pulled her hand back and reached across to my lower neck, by my shoulder instead. She looked over at Honey and reached a hand out, but rather than Honey bolting, she just walked away a little. We agreed to test her, and give her an inch if she earned it. Honey doesn't like this plan, but she agreed to it.

When Honey stopped walking Taylor walked towards her, when Honey would tense, Taylor would lean back and hang out until Honey would relax. It was an interesting dance to watch. I have certainly never met a human like this one before.

After about a half an hour of the dance between Honey and Taylor. Honey allowed Taylor to touch her shoulder. Poor Honey tensed hard, she was trying so desperately to trust, but I don't know that she will ever be able to really trust the humans. I can't say that I blame her, but I love that she was trying. Taylor pet her for a minute or so and then moved slowly away and left. She stopped next to me, winked and said "Thanks for talking to her, Lady." I was a little startled by the comment, but I just huffed like I didn't have any idea what she was talking about.

236's Journal

Grandma likes the Taylor monster, I think. I don't like any of them, but if Grandma says that we need to give this one a chance- I will try.

I can't help that I tense up when the monster's touch me. I am waiting for the blow, the beating, the halter and tubes. The monsters don't change and I am 100% convinced of that. It took awhile for me to get up the nerve to let her touch me. I would try and stay still but then I would get anxious and walk away. After a while Taylor learned that I was nervous and would back off a little and let me just stand there. It seemed like forever, but I eventually gave in and let her touch my shoulder.

It sent a quiver all the way down my spine. Taylor stood there for a bit and just barely put her hand on my shoulder. I couldn't relax, but as my anxiety built I suppose she could feel it, like Grandma had said. She pulled her hand back slowly and walked away. She stopped at Grandma for a moment and said something and then went on to her next horse to harass.

It bothered me all day, I could feel her hand on me and would get shivers from time to time. At the factory people didn't touch horses unless they were taking away our babies, holding us to re-breed, or messing with the tubes and bags to our catheters. I don't understand what this need to touch me is all about. I fear that if we are to be slaughtered; as at the factory, her intent is only to make us easier to handle.

Sherry's Journal

I cried today, big ugly cry. Taylor reported this evening that during the day she had made some progress with Honey. It took time and a lot of patience, but Honey allowed Taylor to approach and to touch her shoulder. While it will still be a long time I think, before Honey really gives us a chance, this is huge news. I am so very grateful for

Taylor who works her magic, and for Honey being willing to give us humans one more chance.

July 25th

There are a lot of volunteers here who handle horses, but Taylor, Sherry and Joe are the only ones who ever come and work with us. I have begun to settle in this place. They brought the old man from next door back, and I have been asking him questions. It looks like they did a good job of cleaning him up too, when they brought him back to the pasture he was all shiny and smelled like soap. As soon as he got back he rolled in the grass and I noticed that he had a brand on his neck. He got up and stretched.

"That's better, it's easier for the predators to find you and sniff you out when you smell like soap." He grinned huge with a missing front tooth.

"Hey, uh...old man?" I called, kind of embarrassed with my frank way.
He half trotted over to the fence, "Well now, I resemble that remark!" He laughed good and hard for a moment and then composed himself, "The name's Buck! And you are?"
"Well, my name is Lady, but everyone calls me Grandma. I would like to talk to you for a while if you don't mind."
"Well, you know, I do keep a pretty busy schedule, but I suppose I could spare a moment." He snort laughed at himself. He was a whimsical old soul, and I liked him instantly.
"You mentioned the other day that the words adoption and sanctuary. What are those?"

"Adoption is when horses take to people and are willing to work with them. The people here decide that you are ready for a new family. People come out and meet you and then after a while they take you home with them to be their horse."

My brow furrowed, Buck noticed and stopped for a moment to let me process. This sounded an awful lot like what Mac had said about the auction house. This sounded a lot like we were still on the road to death.

"Are ya okay, Grandma?" Buck said with genuine concern.

"So this *is* another auction place."

Buck straightened up and suddenly had a very strong presence, not comical, but powerful. "No ma'am! I myself am a mustang and my word is good. This place is not an auction house. This is a haven of sorts. They place horses with families who will take good care of the horses and treat them right. The people here are kind and different from a lot of the humans that I have encountered in my life. I myself, have been here many years, a sanctuary horse, Sherry and Joe pulled me out of a killpen, Taylor spent probably 2 years, bout every day, working with me until I trusted her, they are good people. This is my home until my days are done."

"I too am from a kill pen. If you don't mind my asking, what is that brand on your neck?"

Chapter 7: The Mighty Mustang

Throughout the year our precious wild mustangs are rounded up through violent, terrifying and destructive means. They are split up from their families, branded and placed into pens. For many of them slaughter is where their stories end. This practice regularly costs the lives of hundreds, if not thousands of mustangs every year. Our government currently allows these beautiful creatures, who have done nothing violent or disadvantageous, to be purchased by kill pens for slaughter, in quantity. These animals, who have known nothing other than their wild and beautifully undisturbed families are torn apart and sent to their death.

These, the horses of history, the subject of tales, magic and beauty are being destroyed by our ignorance and the fact that we have come to allow the decimation of our heritage. Buck is one of few which have endured a far less gruesome outcome. Many suffer far more horrific ends. His story only a glimpse of what has become a destructive and continuing disgrace of our inhumane humanity.

Buck smacked his lips and pseudo-suckled, it was obviously not an indicator of a good memory for him. I was embarrassed, "I'm sorry, you don't have to relive your past on my behalf, I didn't mean..."

He cut me off, "No. It's a hard story, but if you don't know about mustangs ma'am, let me introduce you to your heritage." His presence seemed to radiate from within him and he was suddenly quite solid and strong. There was something feral about him- all manifested in a moment. He got a drink of water and began, " I was a stallion, born wild, raised free out on the ranges in Nevada. I had my herd of 8 mares and my children, there were 13 of us in all waiting for 2 more beautiful babies due any day. We mustangs are close knit family groups, and we defend our own with our lives. I was a young stallion, but was establishing my reputation among the tribes as a tribe leader that should be respected."

As Buck beamed, Honey came over and we listened to his story, as little children would; with anticipation and innocent intrigue. He nodded at Honey and continued. "I had led my herd to the watering hole, and was guarding them there, when another Stallion and his tribe came over the hill. This happened from time to time, stallions that controlled watering holes had a better chance of not only keeping their herd mares, but of gaining and building their family tribe in the process. Water means security. The older Stallion approached with his intent to fight being made clear. As he came at me, I rushed towards him, we were preparing for battle when the huge death bird came over the hills.

It swooped low with a terrifying noise and wings that went around in a circle rather than flapping like a normal bird. I have never seen anything like it. The other stallion and I broke our paths and rushed back to our respective tribes. We were now running for our lives. The death bird chased my herd and after a moment I realized that both tribes were running together in extreme panic." Buck stopped and took a breath, his eyes flicked a deep sorrow for a moment before he gathered himself and returned to the story.

"One of my children fell over some brush and broke a leg, his mother tried to go back, but the death bird wouldn't relent and pushed her ever forward. We had to leave him behind. I don't think he made it, I could hear him screaming over the deafening droning of the bird's wings." Buck choked up for a moment and we saw that he was fighting to keep his emotions in check. He took a deep long breath. "The death bird chased us for hours, one of my mares who was anticipating a baby, went down in labor- I don't know if her and my baby are...were okay. The death bird didn't let up, it just kept chasing us. We ended up through a narrow passageway and then heard a loud clang. Then the death bird just flew away, like nothing.

We had been rounded up into small pens, they separated me from my family, cut out my balls, and put a stick on my neck that was so freezing cold that it burned. They put a rope around my neck with a tag and put me in a pen with other horses, one of them was the old stallion- they had done the same thing to him. The stress of the pens and the experience was too much for him though, he and a couple of the mares in one of the other pens died. One from colic, one from I don't know what. My genitals were sore and we were there for about a month, surrounded by people. Another family was brought through the same way, the droning of the death bird and then terrified families, with mom and babies and injured horses all smashed through the chutes and into the pens, sweaty, scared, dehydrated and exhausted.

Eventually I was loaded up into a moving box, I now know as a trailer, and was hauled off- away from all that was familiar. I ended up in a kill pen with 8 other mustangs, none of them were my family- but we all carried the cold fire brand on our necks. We were called 'direct ship' horses, but Sherry and Joe had been visiting that kill pen and trying to rescue horses from slaughter. Four of the mustangs were loaded onto a death trailer, while I and 3 other mustangs were brought here. While I didn't know what the other trailer was then, I have come to learn that those other mustangs, the four that didn't come here; were shortly after probably eaten by humans.

It was scary here, the first year. The second year was better, but we formed our little herd of four and were wary of the people for a long time. They placed us in a pasture together and referred to us as sanctuary horses- we use to be over there," he motioned with his nose, "by the nurse mare foals. I love babies, and they would gather around next to where I was standing at the fence. Joe and Sherry noticed and eventually they started pulling me out of my mustang herd and would put me in with the scared or nervous babies. Over time, my herd died, two from old age. Sherry and Joe sat with each of them while the vet helped them pass on. One died from colic, although she was 30 so I suppose that could be attributed to old age as well. And now it's just me left, and I get to be here next to you fine ladies. At least until there is a baby that needs me or the Spirit calls me home to be with my tribe, running free again." He was far off for a few minutes, in his mind- I assume he was back on his range, a mighty stallion of stallions, with his tribe. He shook his head for a moment and returned to us.

"This place, these people, they are not bad. I have been here 23 years, I am 29 and never has anyone here been harsh, unkind or mean. There is always food and water. They are different here, and I trust them. You should too."

Both Honey and I were a little shocked by his comment. This once great stallion who had been tortured and his family ripped from him, telling us to trust the people. His story was gruesome and terrifying and clearly still held a strong impression of people in general. We stood there quietly for a while, the three of us. He smiled- he wasn't telling us to trust all people, he was telling us that we could trust *these* people.

While the three of us were standing there, Taylor came by. "Well hey there, Buck! Looks like you made some new friends." Buck went trotting over to her, she scratched him and loved on him for a bit and then looked over at us. She was plotting something. "You know what, I have an idea. I'll be right back." She jogged off and was gone for about 15 minutes when she headed back with a halter and lead. Honey and I stood very still, not leaving our little spot at the fenceline. Taylor just looked at us and laughed. She went to Buck's pasture and put the halter on him. "What do ya say old man, you want a herd again?" She gave him a pat on the neck and led him over to our pasture. Honey and I both perked up and were attentive to what was going on. Taylor walked in with Buck, closed the gate and let him loose. She leaned back against the fence, and Buck stood by her for a moment until she half heartedly swung the rope out and said, "Well? Go get em!"

That crazy old coot went thundering through our little pasture like an insane colt- tail in the air, head high, galloping out and around us like he owned the place. He shot by us, hollering at the top of his lungs, "What-da-ya think ladies? Can you handle all this masculinity?!" And laughing at himself, thoroughly entertained by his own jokes.

After he tired himself out he trotted softly over to Taylor and gave her a little nudge, she laughed and pat him a little, "All right old man." She headed out, back to work with other horses in the ranch. Buck came over, all grins. Tired and nearly lame on one hind, but resilient and strong in his way. I was sad for him that he had lost his family all those years ago, but he was one of us now. Somehow, both Honey and I seemed more complete with him here, we weren't as afraid, we weren't as alone. The rest of the day and long into the evening Buck told us stories of his adventures out on the range, of coyotes and lions and mighty battles with other tribe leaders, sunsets, grasslands and long migrations to new feeding grounds. He told us of his children and his herd. Great wonders, loss, trials and stories of overcoming obstacles as a family, as a tribe. It seemed magical, I have never known such stories, a life without people.

What I do know is that today, we became a herd...no...today we became a *tribe, a family.*

Sherry's Journal
Taylor called and asked if she could put Buck in with Lady and Honey. I was a little concerned at first, Buck is nearly 30 and one good kick from a horse the size of Honey could end him. Taylor

assured me that she would stay for awhile and keep an eye on them. Taylor described how they were interacting at the fence and what she was seeing, so I gave the okay. It would be good for the old man to have a herd again. In looking out across the pastures now, I can see them standing all together. They make a funny little herd, but it seems that in putting the three of them together, they have all come a little more alive.

Chapter 8: To Adopt or Not

Rescue organizations are faced with and criticized for this process more than any other. Everything from "it's too hard to adopt from them." to "they could have taken the time to train the horse for such and such." There is every excuse to do it and there is every excuse not to. It is the duty of the rescue to work with the horse, care for their physical and mental needs, advertise them for adoption, go over every adoption application (which for some horses can be hundreds, while other horses have none), make contact with every potential good match, arrange, and rearrange schedules so that people can meet the horse they want to adopt, set aside time for each of those meet and greets, proceed to reference checks, home checks, arranging transport, and follow up calls and visits to make sure that the horse and family are getting on well. This process happens for each horse; and while this goes on, they are still trying to handle, rescue, feed, evaluate, rehabilitate, care for and help other horses that are in their charge.

What they do is a labor of love.

August 1

Since they have introduced Buck into our herd, we are all much
happier. Taylor is here on a regular basis, Buck gets a brushing and
affection first, mostly because he is an attention hog. I have come to
let her approach and handle me without issue. She seems kind and
has not shown any harshness, though I still shy when she reaches out
to pet my face, ever anticipating the blow to the side of the head, but
it doesn't come. Honey still has her doubts but Taylor can now catch
her after about 10 minutes of dancing and a slow approach. My poor
Honey still tenses to the very touch of a hand though. She always
looks over nervously and smiles at me and Buck. I think Taylor is
rather fond of my big friend.

236's Journal

*Buck is a kind soul. While the two of us are from opposite spectrums of
the world; he wild and free, me tied for the near entirety of my life
confined to a standing stall. He and I share a history of decimated
family and destruction at the hands of the monsters. I am glad that he
is now a part of our herd, he has brought a lightness and a joy that I
didn't even realize I was missing. When we first arrived here, it was
all tension with moments of peace and before I even realized the
change, the peace and contentment now outweigh the tension.*

*Taylor comes around every day. I have tentatively given in, though I
cannot honestly say that I trust this monster. I don't know if I will ever
be able to really trust the monsters, though I suppose that I can accept
that not all of them are determined to cause harm. It still takes me*

*time to prepare myself and allow her approach, I am nervous and
afraid that things will change without notice.*

*She is slow with me, and as I convince myself that today will be the day
I will allow myself the trust that both Buck and Grandma now show, I
simply cannot bring myself to give in to that train of thought.
Grandma is no longer fearful, though she does show nervousness when
Taylor moves towards her head too quickly. Taylor even rode her
around the pasture bareback yesterday. They both seemed to enjoy
themselves, although at first it scared me half to death. It wasn't long,
but I think Grandma likes to feel useful.*

Sherry's Journal
One of our long time adopters called me. She is interested in Lady.
Stormy, whom she adopted years ago, recently passed and she is
looking for a companion for her gelding. I tried to suggest another
horse for her, but she saw something in Lady that needed her. We
spoke for a couple of hours because I am concerned about separating
Honey and Lady. With Buck in there, it may actually be okay. So we
agreed to a foster situation to allow us all time to see how each of the
girls will adjust without the other. Denise will come out and spend a
few days just getting to know Lady so that she is at least somewhat
familiar for this timid horse. Taylor was able to get on and ride Lady
around the pasture today, so I think she will transition well, as long as
she and Honey can adjust.

August 2

Today I got another bath, I am settling in I suppose, and finding the
company of both Buck and Taylor pleasant. Of course Honey is my

other half, but the other two are starting to become a nice addition to the day. A volunteer came through and began to groom Buck, I am still not a fan of strangers, so I kept my distance. It was a man and I have learned that men can be fierce and violent without warning. As he approached me I became very nervous and ran to the other end of the pen, Honey sensing my anxiety followed suit and joined me in the corner.

The man seemed unsure of himself but approached us slowly, trying to make nice. Honey feigned a rush but Buck intervened, and came between us and the man, seeking more attention. I was grateful and nodded to Buck, who just smirked ever so slightly.

236's Journal

They sent a different monster to our pen today. He looked like the monster that always took my children, and I stayed far far away from him. He stayed with Buck for about a half an hour before attempting to approach Grandma. She tried to be strong, but I could see that she was nervous. I waited to see what she would do, when she took off I followed her and got between her and the monster. He was agitated and I was terrified that it would turn violent so I rushed at him with my teeth bared. I did not want to engage him, as I had seen what these male monsters are capable of, tearing small babies away from their mothers. They have no heart, I'm not even sure they have a soul. They are just beasts that glean joy from inflicting pain. I am sure that he was using Buck to try and get close to us. Buck says that is not the case, but I have my own experiences that I can attest to. That monster was not going to get the chance to inflict pain on poor Grandma.

August 5

Taylor was back today, and my anxiety was palpable. She had left us in the hands of men, and I wasn't sure how to feel about that. She was her usual chipper self and brought apples. I waited back for a while. She knew something was off, waited at the edge of the feed bin and just watched us for a while. Buck of course, approached and got himself an apple. He made a face and was a little exaggerated in his enjoyment of the fruit, so I approached and allowed the affection.

"Well Lady, I have some good news. We have a foster who would very much like to meet you. If it all goes well, Buck will take good care of your big friend there." I was confused. I don't know what a foster is, so I immediately asked Buck.

While he had heard the term, he wasn't sure what it was either. I tried not to think about it, but it was at the back of my mind all day. I still have good days and bad days, but today was definitely not a good day. I didn't mention the conversation to Honey, I don't need to scare her if there is no reason to do so.

August 6

Today was the day. Taylor came in the morning and took me out to the wash rack. Honey was nervous, but Buck reassured her and she settled down. While she didn't freak out she did stand at the gate and call to me. "Grandma! What is happening?" All I could respond was that I didn't know, but I thought it would be okay.

Taylor put me in a stall and proceeded to brush me out, she talked to me the whole time. "You know Lady, this could be an opportunity to have a family. Denise seems really nice. She saw your picture on our website and called about you." Taylor kept talking, but I could hear Honey calling for me. I drifted away a little bit.

I remembered at the kill pen, there were babies that were alone. They were pacing and calling for their momma's, some of them were so small, skinny, dirty. What made my life more valuable than theirs? Why am I in this place, being fed well, brushed and with a herd, small though it is. I am content here, but I often think about those babies. Those poor little things, terrified, alone. I try not to picture what comes next for them but I can't help but see them packed onto a trailer, scared off of the trailer. A gun to their tiny little heads and then slaughtered-like they are nothing. My heart breaks every time I think of those small ones, and I feel guilty for being grateful that I am here...breathing...alive.

After a while, a woman came. She was older, soft, she reminded me of the wife of my owner. Taylor climbed out of the stall and greeted her. "Denise, this is Lady. She is a little shy and untrusting when you first meet her, but once she warms up to you she is sweet and kind as can be." The woman, Denise, approached with a quiet confidence. Rather than reach to touch me, she brought her hand out and allowed me to make the decision to make contact or not. I was tentative, but I reached out to the hand that was hanging in the air in front of me and checked it.

"Hello, Lady." Denise said in a quiet and calm voice that was meant to be reassuring, but I was just not sure about this whole situation. "I would very much like for us to become friends." She slid her hand up and to the side of my neck where she gave me a firm scratch. It was gentle and kind, but she had the rough hands of someone who works outside a lot. I enjoyed the little bit of attention while the two women talked.

By the end of the visit, both women were nodding and Denise said, "I'll see you later, Lady." Taylor gave me a gentle pat on the neck and walked me back to my family. Honey checked me and was showing her usual loving concern for me, while Buck was off happily munching grass.

236's journal

They took her away. Taylor came and took her away! I was so afraid that they were going to hurt her, that they were going to kill her. I didn't know what to expect, but I was terrified for my friend. When she came back, she had the smell of a different beast on her. She said that she met a monster (she called it a woman) who wants to be her friend. Grandma said that the woman seemed kind, but I just don't trust the monsters. They are plotting something and I don't like it. First with the man monster the other day and now this.

I don't know what is going on, but at the factory, horses would disappear- though I suppose the horses at the factory now say the same thing about me. I don't know why I am not dead and on someone's table right now- the seven girls that came in with me are. They were the only family I had known for 14 years, such beautiful lives, so fully wasted. I don't want Grandma to disappear.

Sherry's Journal

We did a trial run with Honey and Lady today, to see if there would even be a chance that this would work without Honey becoming unhandleable and regressing. Taylor took Lady out to get her ready for her visit. I watched Honey and her reactions to the situation from a distance. I was getting more excited. Honey was initially very nervous, but our intuitive little Buck came alongside her and she settled. She was not completely comfortable with it as I could see, but she was okay. It gives me reason to hope. While I am not typically an emotional person outwardly, this mare brings out tears in me more often that I care to admit.

August 8

I didn't sleep well last night, neither did Honey. Both of us were up and down throughout the night, Buck sleeps deeply. I sometimes think that in his dreams, he is back out on the range with his herd, running free, with his family in tact. Perhaps that is why he sleeps so deeply, because in his dreams he has reason to stay sleeping.

I worry for Honey, I know that Buck says that we are safe here, but Honey is sensitive and her flashbacks are getting bad- she is scared and angry for days afterwards. I know that she is very loving and does not take anything for granted, but I am glad that she can lay down and sleep. I know that laying down is a special thing for her. I could not imagine what she went through in her lifetime. And here I am, just an old ranch mare that was whooped on, we were all whooped on. I was discarded just for being "old" I don't feel worthy of the friendship of these two mighty survivors. I suppose what binds our odd little herd is that we are all discarded.

236's Journal

I was looking around at the horses in this place, while it was dark, while everything was quiet. There are so many horses here. Each with a story; like mine, like Grandma's, like Buck's. Each of us intercepted from death, destruction, trauma. Some of the horses are sleeping, some are standing guard over their herds, though quietly, comfortably, knowing that danger is not near. I have had to learn how to be a horse. And while that seems a funny concept, that is the one that is on my mind tonight. In my fourteen years, I have never been a horse; only a piece of machinery that happens to feel. We were not social together in the factory, we were bound together in our plight. I considered them my family. While we did form some relationships, we were not close, we did not run and gallop and touch each other. We were simply present in the same hell.

Here, things are different. This is all so new to me, touching, eating and grazing. Hell, I didn't even know what grass was until just recently. It's still so fresh, this life without wires or tubes or hearing the screams of horses in pain. When Buck told his story, I could not relate to his freedom, only his loss. We are an odd few, we three. Buck who had never had any interaction with monsters before death came knocking, Grandma who had worked with them side by side for many years, anad me who has only ever endured pain at their hands. I had no idea that so many horses led so many different lives.

*And yet, at the hands of **these** monsters, we have all ended up here-together. We all ended up destined for death and cast off as being useless for nothing other than to feed the monsters, but **these** monsters*

decided that our lives meant something, even mattered maybe. I will
try again in the morning... to be a horse.

August 9

Taylor came early in the morning, and as per usual she has taken it upon herself to be the bearer of hay and treats. She brought apples and I could smell them before she even got to the gate. Buck was just waking up and was still curled into a warm comfortable position in the grass. To my surprise it was Honey who headed off first. She looked terrified but determined. As Taylor entered our field, I thought perhaps that Honey was going to bowl her over. Taylor was latching the gate when Honey put her head down and nudged the bag of apples.

Taylor turned a little too quickly, not realizing who it was. Honey startled and bolted backwards a few paces. She stayed near. "Well, HI!" Taylor laughed a little and then turned absolutely soft towards my large friend. She got an apple out of her bag and offered it to Honey, who took it whole mouthed and chewed graciously while Taylor stroked her neck. Honey was still tense through her neck, you could see her fighting against her own fear, but her eyes were soft and she let Taylor stroke her fur while she continued to munch on apple after apple. Taylor was crying and smiling, Honey did as much as she could do and then quietly walked away to get a drink of water. Buck and I just looked at each other for a barely perceptible moment and then Buck heaved himself from the ground and leaned himself back into a long stretch. I noticed that he was surprisingly muscular for an old man, built more like a tank than a horse.

"Looks like Denise is really excited to spend time with you , Lady."
Taylor came over to me and offered an apple and a scratch on the
shoulder. Denise. She seemed like an okay human. I recalled that she
smelled like my owner's wife, and that woman was always kind to
me.

Buck, Honey and I spent the day exchanging stories. Buck of his wild
adventures out on the range and the horror of the BLM Corrals.
Honey told of her children, and of the terrifying hell where she lived.
I told of the cows, the work on the mountains, and shared the
campfire stories that I heard from other horses on the picket line in
the evening. It was a calm day as we ate, grazed and napped in the
cool grass through this hot August heat.

None of us anticipating the changes that would come.

Sherry's Journal
I was sitting on the porch drinking my coffee, watching the morning
unfold. Horses in pastures just waking up, the little ones running and
playing. Taylor likes to come early to work with Honey and Lady. I
watched as Honey headed in Taylor's direction, determined. I
thought, for a moment, that Honey was going to run Taylor over,
but she stopped and nudged at a bag of goodies. I was so proud of
her, that mare is trying so hard to heal.

Chapter 9:Shift

The hard transition to a foster or adoption home can be rough, on both the horse and the individual/family that has brought the rescue home. It takes patience. We forget sometimes that many of these animals have been passed around so much that they tend to shut down. I have seen it take months, and in some cases up to a year, for a rescue or abused horse to come out of their shell with a new family.

We forget sometimes that while we are prepared to offer them the best home and the most love they have ever received; we are often the 4th, 5th, 20th home they have seen in their short lives. Horses create very tight family bonds and their past has a far greater impact, than just what can be seen on their skin. Some horses are glad and excited for new friends and adventures, while others need time to process that they are not being discarded and that it is okay to *be*.

August 10

The heat came early. By feeding time we were already seeking shade.
About 10 o'clock Taylor came with Denise not far behind her. They
came into the pasture. Buck, as usual was the first one to greet them
at the gate. He relished the scratches and attention, sniffed around
pockets and investigated this new woman who had come in to our
pen. Honey followed me tentatively, she had just began to warm up
to Taylor and I was unsure how she would do with this new friend.

Though she kept me between herself and this new person she did
reach over the top of me and snag the carrot that was offered. Petting
from this new one was out of the question though. Taylor came
around me slowly and waited for Honey to signal that she was okay
with the approach. Denise spent time petting me and gave me
chunks of carrots while Taylor stood quietly with Honey, softly
stroking her neck from time to time. I was proud of my friend, she
had come a long way. I don't know that she will ever give herself over
fully to trusting, but she tolerates Taylor and is trying to give her the
benefit of the doubt. I don't fully trust people either, but at least my
large friend for the moment, does not seem to be afraid to live.

Denise spoke to me and was quiet and tender in her attention. She
grabbed one of the halters from the fence and stood quietly about
three feet away from me. I was nervous and rocked back on my
haunches a little bit, but she didn't approach. She simply stood there,
speaking softly, "It's up to you, I know you're scared, but you can
trust me."
Trust. My lips pursed for a moment. I hate that the humans use this
word. "Trust" seems to be a very common though misguided word

among the humans. I do not *know* you or who I can *trust*. As I was trying to decide what to do Buck decided to be his comical self and walked up behind Denise, jamming his head into the halter all by himself.

I snorted, Honey looked slightly disgusted, and the two women were laughing hysterically. Buck picked his head up, halter half on and hanging from his face. He looked utterly ridiculous and trotted off with his little half limp, completely and perfectly full of himself. Eventually the halter fell off and he picked it up in his teeth, started galloping around and shaking the halter vigorously. I have never met a horse who so fully entertains himself.

Once the two women had composed themselves from their fit of laughter, Denise went back and got another halter from the fence. Buck looked over, halter still in his mouth and Denise just giggled, "Don't you dare, mister." grinning widely. Buck just stood over in the shade and continued to play with his newly won prize. Denise looked over to me, carefully and slowly I approached. She very calmly put the halter on me and began petting me. She found that belly scratch spot that is always so hard to reach and I stretched out and rocked back and forth to give her better assistance in her efforts.

Honey watch it all with great interest, and then bumped Taylor's shoulder a little. "Oh really?" Taylor laughed. Cautiously she ran her hand down Honey's side to the belly spot. Honey tensed hard, but Taylor began to scratch her, gently at first and then a little more vigorously. Honey's upper lip went WILD. Eventually the heat was too much for anyone to bear, so the two women left and we horses huddled together in the shade.

236's Journal

*I am not even sure how to describe the weird day. Taylor brought
another monster with her that seemed to take great interest in
Grandma, this must have been the "new friend" that she spoke of
before. Taylor made her way over to me and while I am not quite
ready to trust her, we seem to have come to an understanding between
ourselves. I am not wholly afraid of that one. I tried to show a little
more patience with the monsters and followed Grandma over to the
new lady. Using Grandma as a buffer I took a carrot from the new
lady and then left.*

*Buck was feisty and I think maybe he is getting too much alfalfa. Other
than the gimp and the grey you would not know from his actions today,
that he turns 30 next month. Crazy old coot. If that is how normal
horses act, I'm not sure I want to even try. Ha.*

*After a while the new lady started scratching Grandma's belly,
Grandma started swaying back and forth and looked like she was
going to fall down from pure enjoyment. I watched this go on for a
while, I know that spot and it's so hard to get myself. I tried to employ
Taylor's assistance by nudging her. I am not the one who typically
makes contact so I was a little nervous about it, but Grandma seemed
to be loving the spot scratch. Taylor moved slowly and I still could not
help but tense every muscle in my body and prepare to flee. I fought it,
fought myself, and then she got to the spot that itches and Oh My God!
I have never felt anything so enjoyable. I stretched my head way out
and my lip started to quiver, I just couldn't help myself. I felt
ridiculous, but I didn't even care. It was the same feeling as I got the*

first time I got to lay down and sleep, at the kill pen, the day I met Grandma.

Oh it was bliss. I was totally into it for a few minutes, and then my anxiety got the best of me and I took off. I looked at Taylor and then at Grandma, I felt a little ashamed that I couldn't just give in. Taylor saw my worry, "it's all right Honey, small steps love, small steps." She came towards me and then stopped a few feet away until I gave her the signal that she could come closer. She walked over to stroke my neck once, placed her head against my neck and said, "Good girl." I felt her tears through my fur. She stepped back and where I once thought she was baring her teeth, I now know this is a sign that she is happy with me, she smiled. I dropped my head and let the tension release. I had never had a monster who was proud of me.

Buck's Journal

I don't typically write. But I have seen horses do it from time to time and at nearly 30, I figure why not try something new. The trainer, Taylor, brought a new person to the pasture with her today. I know what that means and I watch carefully. Everyone seems to think I am just some old fool, but I am still as sharp as I was when I was leading my tribe on the range. The new woman went to Grandma.

Honey and Taylor seem to be growing closer and while I would by no means quantify them as bonded I am glad that Honey is learning to be a horse. She is only 14 and still just a baby, with much to learn. The new woman went and got a halter after a while and attempted to convince Grandma to come to her. Everyone in the pasture, both mares and both people were trying to pretend to be relaxed, but I could see the tension in the shoulders and the belly. My mares use to get that way when another stallion would challenge me. While I could tell that this woman and Grandma were not going to fight, it was a challenge nonetheless. So I turned on all of my charm! I decided to halter myself but it fell off, so I decided to pretend it was a snake and threw it around and played with it. I stomped it a couple times for good measure and then continued on to the delight of all my adoring fans (except Honey). The mood lightened and everyone relaxed.

Tonight Grandma and Honey seemed to be in good spirits and I joined in the lightness, but I had a heavy heart that I was trying to hide. I have seen this type of day before. Our little herd will be broken soon.

Sherry's Journal

Honey is making progress in leaps and bounds with Taylor. I was working with some of the foals in a different pasture when I heard laughter. I looked up to see Buck working his usual antics of exuberance and then watched as the scene unfolded before my eyes. Taylor scratching Honey's belly and the mare was LOVING it! I couldn't believe what I was seeing and once again this mare brought out tears of joy in me. One of the fillies came over and nudged me because I was snot bubble crying, I had to reassure her that I was fine. I wish I had a camera to capture that moment. It makes all the effort and struggle and everything worth it. Moments like that are why we do what we do. These are the things that renew our passion.

August 11

This morning Denise and Taylor were back. I should have known when Buck stayed back a little bit, that something was off. Denise and Taylor came in to the pasture, just as they had yesterday. Denise took a halter from the fence and came near, but waited without fully approaching. I was becoming more at ease with this woman, but I was still a little bit nervous, as I did not know her well. I approached cautiously and she haltered me gently. Taylor opened the gate and Denise led me out. They led me across the ranch and I could hear Honey once again calling. I was quiet, as I assumed that I was being led to the stalls again for an afternoon of interaction and attention, but this time was different.

They led me past the stalls, and I turned to look over assuming that we had simply over shot, but Denise softly reinforced our direction, "This way, Lady." As I turned to look forward again, there awaiting me was a trailer. I froze. I thought we were past this. I thought I was entitled to live, breathe, be. I flashed to the kill pen, the horses being forced and packed into the trailers. I considered my situation. The trailer I was facing was large and could easily accomodate 3 horses. I had a halter and a lead. Maybe this was different? I exhaled deeply and tentatively loaded onto the trailer. It took a few minutes before I heard the engine of the truck start its low soft temblor. I was the only horse on the trailer. I remembered my herd and called as loudly as I could, "I'm sorry." My own voice echoing in the trailer. I don't know if my dear Honey heard me. Goodbye my sweet loves.

After about a half an hour drive, the truck came to a bumpy halt. I waited, breathing shallow, nervous...scared. As the trailer door opened I saw Denise, smiling softly and trying to reassure me. "Easy dear, you're all right." She untied the lead and led me to a large paddock. To my left there was another paddock, with another horse in it. Denise walked me to the right hand paddock and took me inside, she walked me over to where the water was, and over to where there was hay in a trough. She took my halter and lead off. I looked at her, betrayed, heartbroken, lost. "I know dear, but if you will have me, I would love to be your friend and you are welcome to be here as long as you like. I know you miss your friends, but I think you are wonderful and hope that you come to find me tolerable." She reached out to give me a soft pat on the neck, which I shied away from. She recoiled as though I had kicked her, it was not a reaction I was familiar with. As she turned to leave I followed, hoping that she would load me back onto the trailer and take me back to my herd. But that was not the case, she turned to the other horse and said something, and then she was gone for a long time.

The horse in the paddock next to me spoke gently, "Hi." I turned my head sharply, with my ears pinned and rushed the fence.
"Go AWAY!" I screamed. "I just want to go home!"
This gelding nextdoor smiled, quietly and without malice he asked, "And where is that?"
As I was about to snap at him, I stopped. Where *is* home? I had the same one for twenty years, and then I didn't have one at all, just passed around. I ignored him instead of responding. I began to pace at the front gate and along the fence. I was worried about Honey. The gelding kept trying to talk to me, but I ignored him and continued along the fence line. It was getting blazing hot out, but I didn't relent, by 11am I was frothy and dripping sweat. The neighbor gelding yelled, it wasn't even a word, it was just a noise. But there must have been some sort of agreement between him and that woman, because she came outside. Saw me shaking, pacing, covered in sweat and came directly over. "Okay Blue, I got her from here." What the hell did that mean? She came in with a halter and I bolted. Not again! She was quiet about her approach, I was exhausted and

getting more overheated and angry by the minute. She stood quietly, with the halter which prompted me to stand still, ready to react to any move, except I had sweat getting in my eyes, and I wasn't sure my legs would actually keep up with my desire. That woman came at me carefully. She haltered me and walked me along a path near the house that had a lot of shade and trees. Once I was breathing close to regular, she tied me to a large shady tree in the grass. She walked away for a moment and came bath with a hose and a sweat scraper. She turned it on very low and tested the water. "Sorry sweetheart, it's still a little hot, it'll take a minute." After a little bit she turned the hose towards me, she began at my front feet, working slowly up my shoulder and neck, and then back down to my butt and my hinds.

She used her fingers to scratch the wet side, wet me down again slowly, methodically on one side before switching to the other. When we were all finished she turned off the water and came at me with the sweat scraper, I instinctively shied from the motion. I was too hot to notice what it was and for a moment thought she was going to hit me with a stick. She gently pet me for a moment and then began scraping the excess water off of my body. Afterwards, we headed back to the paddock. Rather than turning me loose, this time she led me over to the shade, which covered a large area in both paddocks. She climbed up, sat on the fence and stayed there, attached to me, in the hot shade.

We sat there into the night. She never left, but would occasionally walk me over to the water to drink and then we would return to our post. Once the sun went down, she finally let me go and returned to the house. The neighbor gelding came over, but didn't bother to engage me, he just stood close, quiet.

I allowed the darkness and the night to envelope me.

236's Journal

*They took her! They came this morning and they took her away! I
called for her all morning, I paced, but there was nothing. I...I don't
know what to do! I failed her! They took her to slaughter and I let them
do it. They got me to let my guard down and I let them take her. I
heard a faint call, she said she was sorry, and then there was a truck
and they TOOK her. I have lost everyone! What have I done that the
monsters have to take EVERYONE!?*

*Buck has been trying to console me, but he is failing, not because of him,
but because of **them**. I will not give in again. I just....what am I going
to do now? They've killed Grandma. All I can see is my mother, in my
mind, being drug out of the aisle by a tractor. I can't lose this one, she
was the only family that I had. I don't know what to do. I don't know
how to get her back.*
My stomach hurts.

Buck's Journal

*It was sooner than I thought it would happen. They came for Grandma
early. Honey was calling all day, pacing the fence and crying. I tried to
tell her that Grandma was fine, that she wasn't headed to slaughter.
When she asked me if I had seen any of the horses who left on trucks,
recently, I could not say that I had. I tried my best. I hope Grandma is
doing better than Honey. I feel like I should have warned them, but I
don't know that it would have helped. Honey doesn't look well, she
didn't eat and she barely drank anything all day. They even tried to*

sedate her, but they couldn't get anywhere close, she was too upset. Once Grandma was loaded and on her way, Taylor came back to the pasture, but Honey pinned her ears, kicked out and ran. That big girl thunders pretty quickly. I can hear her moaning in the corner, even now.

Oh Shit.

Chapter 10: Hard Battles and Life Lessons

Transitioning into a new life can be difficult. Taking chances, overcoming fears. We struggle and we strive for those things which we are passionate about. Sometimes we are told to quit, sometimes we want to quit. There are trials, struggles, failures and successes every step of the way. Some of our battles are hard won, and some of our struggles are detrimental.

Those of us who are passionate about horses and rescue are constantly faced with the battle between our heartbreak and our desire. We are passionate about helping animals that have issues and our struggles and successes always hugely affect the animals that we work with on regular basis. Bringing them out of a kill pen is a matter of life and death for them.

Rehabilitating them, can sometimes be a matter of life and death for us.

August 12

I did not sleep much last night, but my legs were too sore and tired to pace. The gelding next door kept a quiet vigil over me through the night. He would sleep for a while, but he seemed like he was waiting. For what, I don't know.

That woman was out before the sun was even up. "Oh sweetheart, didn't you eat at all?" She looked quite genuinely concerned. Her brow furrowed and she walked away into the barn for a little bit. When she came out, she brought out a pail with her. I could smell apple, molasses and a plethora of other scents that made my mouth water. She set the pail in my pasture and went to tend to the neighbor horse.

I looked over, I was so distraught yesterday that I hadn't even noticed him, other than the fact that he was there and trying to talk to me. He was *beautiful*, a large blue roan, thick, muscular and tall, with just a little bit of feather to his feet. After that woman left, I tried to sound interested, but I didn't have the strength of heart to pull it off. Without even lifting my head or really looking over I asked him, "What is your name?"

"Blue." His voice was gentle and deep, it would have been soothing if I had not been so distraught.
"Where are you from?" Again I didn't sound convincing, even to myself, but he was kind and answered my questions as they came.
"Well, that's a tougher question than my name." I brought my head up and he suddenly had my intent focus.

"Why?" I was in fact, now very interested in his answer and he knew it.

"Well, I was born to what they call a PMU mare. They took me away when I was just a baby. I was 2 months old when I ended up at the kill pen, they sent me there with twenty three other foals, about my age- we were all between 2 and 4 months old. I didn't know where my momma was, I didn't know who these people were. I didn't know any of the horses, even the other babies weren't familiar and we were split up into separate pens throughout the place. Three of the babies that came with me died during the few days we were there. I kept getting slammed into the fences by the other horses. Some people came and saw me, if I remember correct their names were Sherry and Joe. They were good people. They took myself and eight other foals out of those pens. They saved our lives.

We were at the rescue place for a long time, they started us out on milk from a bucket, and then pellets, and eventually, when we were old enough we started eating hay. They took good care of us. When I was about eight months old, Denise adopted me and one of the older horses, a mare that they had there. So to answer your question. I am from a total of four different places. Although this one seems to be my permanent residence as I have been here for ten years."

He was not patronizing in his answer, but thorough and thoughtful. I considered his words for a long time before asking my next question. "You said that you were adopted with another horse. Where is she?"

"There." He motioned to a field where a small tree had been planted, there was a halter hanging on the tree. " We lost her three months ago to cancer. Denise did everything she could, but there was nothing more to be done. Momma was hurting and Denise sat with her the whole time that the vet was here. The vet gave her a shot to put her to sleep and never wake up. They planted the tree over her grave the next day. She was 32." He stopped, and was quiet for a long time, solemn and far off, no doubt remembering the only mother he had really known. After a long silence, he looked over to me, "Your name is Lady?"

I choked up a little in my answer, "Yes, but my tribe called me Grandma."

Buck's Journal

Last night I heard Honey moaning, I thought she was just sad that Grandma was gone, but when I looked over she was on the ground and looked in pain. I rushed over to her and asked her what was wrong. She just grimaced and looked at me. I started for the gate and hollered at the top of my lungs. I screamed for the people for what seemed like hours, though it was honestly only about 5 minutes. By the time Joe came out with a flashlight my throat was sore and gravelly. "Buck! What the hell is going on?"

I ran to Honey and back to the gate, back and forth. About my third trip to the gate he followed me in, his flashlight beam searching the pasture. When his beam hit her, she was rolling. It was getting bad fast. "Okay, okay." He said to me. He got his phone out and called Sherry, "It's Honey and I am going to need your help." He didn't even elaborate, he was on the phone with the vet moments later. "We need you out at the ranch 5 minutes ago. Honey is colicing and getting bad fast."

"Buck!" I heard Honey call. "What is happening?" She was terrified and her voice tremored.

"You are colicing Honey, you need to try and calm down and you have to let the people help."

She snapped at me, "They aren't getting anywhere near me, they killed Grandma and they aren't getting...ahhhh." She began to thrash. "They aren't killing me!" She gasped.

"Honey! If you don't let them help you, you WILL die here."

*Sherry was coming into the pasture with a halter. You could see that she was nervous, but she was absolutely determined. "Turn off your light Joe." Her husband turned towards her absolutely defiant and perplexed. This is honestly the most dangerous mare they have on the property right now and she had just asked him to put them in complete darkness. But Sherry is a smart one, she knows that **we** can see. "Joe, we don't have time for this, PLEASE." Her husband complied and we were immersed in nothing but moonlight.*

She gave her eyes a moment to adjust. Sherry had often walked the pastures at night when she couldn't sleep, her eyes were better than most humans. I had come to the conclusion that this woman may actually be part horse. She walked over to me, "Buck I'm going to need your help." She placed her hand on my shoulder and we walked together towards where Honey was struggling. I put my nose down next to Honey's nose, Sherry moved very slowly, but with a efficiency and urgency. In a few seconds she had the halter over Honey's head and secure. "Okay Buck, she needs to get up."

Honey was in a lot of pain, and I could see that Sherry that was trying to be as gentle as she possibly could with this very large, very scared and reactive mare. She placed a little bit of tension on the line, "Honey, sweetheart, you need to get up." Sherry looked at me. She knew this mare didn't trust her and Sherry was pleading with her eyes for me to help save this stubborn mare.

"Honey," I was still nose to nose with her, "You need to get up." I nudged her a little.
"They aren't going to kill me!" her bellow echoed into the night.
"You stupid cow!" I snapped at her," if you don't get up I will kill you." I felt bad for saying it, but she was dying where she lay and I knew that if she didn't get up soon it would only end in tragedy. I struck her with a front hoof. "Get up!" I struck her again, not hard enough to hurt her, but hard enough to make a point. Sherry was crying and pulling on the lead. I cried and choked out, "I'm Sorry." This time I walked around and stuck her HARD in the hip.

She slammed forward and got up. She tried to go down again, but I got my body in next to hers and kept her up while Sherry tried to get her walking. Together we got Honey moving. When the vet arrived Sherry hesitated, and Honey went down again. The vet was moving fast, into the back of his truck, meds loaded into a shot. Even though there was no light and the mare was beginning to thrash again, he timed it perfectly and when she came upright a little bit, he snuck in, got the shot in the vein and administered a pain med and a sedative. That man is magic I have no doubt.

After a few moments, Honey settled. After another few moments we were able to get her up again and the vet gave her fluid through an IV, and checked her over, did his thing. He stayed there to monitor her for a few hours, until she started coming out of the sedation. He and Joe talked for a few minutes and then he was gone. Joe came over and told Sherry that the vet had said to monitor Honey about every hour for the next few hours. He and Sherry argued quietly for a few moments and then Joe left. Sherry stayed all night, with that lead rope attached to Honey. She sat on the grass next to the tired mare, and stayed with us all day today, never leaving Honey's side.

In the morning, when Taylor arrived she ran into the pasture and then approached Honey with as much care as she could. "Oh my sweet girl!" She was sobbing. She slowly sat down next to Honey and began stroking her shoulder. "I'm so sorry, love." Honey would have fought the attention, but she was pretty scuffed up and sore from the thrashing and pain the night before. Both women stayed there, in our pasture all day. By the evening Sherry was exhausted, and Taylor convinced her to go in and get some sleep.

Taylor stayed, continuing to care for and check Honey throughout the night. She would stroke her neck, walk her around the pasture, and give her water from a pail that she had brought back from one of her bathroom runs earlier in the day. She had also brought the needed stuff to clean Honey's wounds, but didn't yet impress herself upon the mare to that extent. I tried to keep my distance a little bit. I felt bad for yelling at Honey and striking her so hard. I hope she understands, I only meant to help. She is my friend and I didn't want her to die.

Sherry's Journal

We were at the kill pen all day yesterday. Taylor oversaw Lady's transfer and monitored Honey during the day. Honey was upset and regressed, running from Taylor. We decided to give her one more day before reconsidering Lady's adoption. Joe and I had only been home for about 15 minutes before we heard a commotion out in the pastures. Joe grabbed a flashlight and headed out to see what was going on. A few minutes later my phone rang and Joe sounded terrified, "It's Honey, she's down, it's bad. " That was all. I don't remember if I hung up on him or if he hung up on me, but I was out the door with shoes untied and on the phone with to vet as I ran. The line was busy and I thought maybe Joe was trying to call him too. Honey had been making progress but this could be deadly for any of us, she is by far the most reactive and dangerous mare we have here right now.

As I approached I could see Joe with his flashlight shining on Honey, she was real bad. I grabbed a halter and tried to walk run towards the back of the pasture where Honey was thrashing. Buck came over and I yelled at Joe to turn off his flashlight. He wanted to fight me, but it was easy for me to see in the dark and the horses would be calmer without a blinding light casting scary shadows. Joe reluctantly complied. I called on Buck for assistance and he walked with me and placed his nose down by Honey's face. I don't even know how, because I was just too focused and panicked, but I got a halter on Honey. I hoped that Buck would understand, so I told him that she needed to get up. I cried the whole time. It broke my heart not only to ask but to watch and be a part of. I pulled on the lead, Buck went over to Honey to comfort her a moment and then kicked her repeatedly until she stood up. When the vet got there Honey went down again. Bless that man, in the darkness, ignoring the danger, he

124

was able to get her comfortable enough to stop thrashing and eventually get up. He worked quickly and was able to get her right, but I stayed with her for the rest of the night to make sure that she was going to be okay. This poor mare has been through enough already. I felt guilty, but was glad that everyone was safe and that she was going to hopefully be okay. Taylor showed up in the morning and we took turns sitting with Honey. This evening she finally argued her way into sending me in the house. I called Denise to check on Lady, who had also had a rough transition, but was doing okay now. It's been nearly 48 hours since I have slept, and I think it's time for me to go lay down. Taylor will stay with Honey tonight and I will check on her in the morning.

August 12

That woman brought us hay and grain this morning, she groomed Blue for a while and then came into my paddock. I watched as she cleaned and was just generally around. She would look at me and smile, but she didn't interact, she just continued on with her work. As I ate she approached me, I brought my head up out of the feeder and just looked at her, leaned back a little and prepared to leave. She read my intent and stopped, she sighed and walked away, looking a little defeated. After about an hour she came back out with a hat on and carrying a chair. She came into my paddock, set herself up in the shade of my shelter and proceeded to sit and begin reading a book. What is with this woman?

I looked over to Blue, who just smiled, "She likes you. She isn't going to give up, you know." He continued eating. I realized that this woman was smarter than most as our water was in the shade, about a foot from her. The temperature was climbing and it was starting to get very hot out, we were well over a hundred degrees. I withstood it as long as I could, but around 1 o'clock I went in and got a drink. I kept close watch on the woman, but she didn't move or show anything other than being concentrated on her book. I stood in the shade, about a foot from her, and rested through the heat of the day. My mind wandered, my sorrow about Mac came to the forefront for a moment. He was a good horse, kind and didn't deserve to die. If he had been given the time to rest and heal, he would have still been a good horse, instead of bleeding out and being skinned. He didn't deserve that. I thought of Bert, he was a kind and jolly horse that reminded me somewhat of Buck. I thought of Honey and the babies that she had lost to slaughter, but then something occurred to me. It couldn't be possible.

I looked up, out of my midday dreaming, "Blue." I leaned over the fence, and Blue looked up. "You said you were a PMU foal. This may seem an odd question, but do you remember the number that was branded on your mother's hip?"

"Wow, okay yeah I wasn't really expecting that. Um, well maybe. I think about her all the time, and I remember that it was there, but it was so long ago. Let me think for a minute." Blue stared off into blankness for a long while. You could see him remembering his mother, his expressions changing throughout the memory. He looked like a lifetime had passed, "I'm sorry, I can see it, but I can't remember for sure." He began to walk away, but turned with a furrowed brow and a curiosity laden voice, "Why do you ask?"

I explained to him about Honey, but didn't mention what her number was. Since they had come from the same kill pen, that there was a good chance they had come from the same PMU facility. There was a very small chance that perhaps, my friend was his mother. "Wait! What did your mother look like?"

There were two other PMU mares that were in the same pen as Honey at the kill pen. Honey was a chestnut marked 236, there was a big bay mare I think her number was 171, but I wasn't really paying all that much attention. There was a third mare and as I was seeing her in my mind eye, Blue began to describe his mother.

He lit up for a moment. "She was a beautiful chestnut mare. She had a sweet face and the softest eyes. She would scratch my butt to make me kick and then we would laugh like there wasn't a care in the world. She had a small white spot on her belly about the size of an apple. She had a..."
I continued for him. "White star and a white leg that came about to her hock....her number was 189..." He looked at me with sheer surprise.
Excitedly he exclaimed, "Your friend is my mother?!" But then he noticed the heartbreak in my face and that I was crying.
"No, sweet boy. I'm so sorry." My voice cracked and I choked on the words, "But my friend knew your mother. They came to the kill pen together. I'm so very sorry, I shouldn't have brought all that back for you. Blue I'm so sorry."

He looked at me with deep sorrow in his eyes. "It shouldn't bother me this much, you know. It's been years. I mean they threw me away, why would my mother be any different. I just...I always..." He began to cry and every part of me broke for this young horse. It was my fault and I now couldn't go back or make it right. His mother had been one of the horses loaded onto the death trailer when Honey, myself and the other two were loaded on a trailer to life. I had not meant to cause this poor boy harm. Denise could sense that something was off, when she turned I startled and shot backwards a few paces. She looked over at Blue and his body language was evident enough, even for a human. She climbed over the railing and went to him. She gently pet him along his neck.

"My boy, what's the matter?" She soothed him and caressed his neck and face, placed her body up against his gently, shoulder to shoulder. Her approach was very *equine.* He leaned into her and the two of them stood there together for a long time, until Blue began to regain himself. Denise went and got a halter and a lead and took him out to the big tree that she had tied me to, the first day. She disappeared for a bit and came back with brushes. As she groomed him gently, she sang softly. "Oh though a person I may be, the horse of course, is what sets me free. My heart can only sing to a ho-of beat, and that's why this song is for you and me. Oh my sweet boy, horse of my soul, oh my sweet boy life brings us hardship, life brings us hope. Mane and tail and thundering hooves, life is always better with a horse of course. Oh though a person I may be, the horse is of course, what sets me free."

As she sang, Blue settled into a deep relaxation. A reassurance that though life was hard in the past that they would get through this together. It was a beautiful thing to watch the two of them. I thought maybe, I could try to give this woman another chance. Part of me felt that, if I were happy here I was abandoning my herd- Buck and Honey.

236's Journal

It was a rough two days. I was so tore up about Grandma leaving that I barely ate, didn't drink any water and then got myself into a bad way the other night. Buck called for help and the monsters came in the darkness. Sherry...helped me. She was gentle and kind, but persistent. She was certainly kinder than Buck, but I understand why he did what he did. He kept his distance all through yesterday, I know he felt bad for having to be so rough with me. I was glad that he was there. I know had he not been there I would have died for sure.

I don't think the people here want to kill me, otherwise why didn't they just let me die there? Taylor and Sherry sat with me all day the next day and Taylor stayed through the following night. Today, she tried to turn the hose on and get me wet, but I have never had a monster do that to me before and I totally freaked out, it made it feel like my leg was bleeding and I couldn't take it. I pulled back hard and she lost her footing. I thought she was going to be mad and hit me so I tried to run and ended up dragging her halfway across the pasture. She never let go of the line. When I finally stopped, she didn't approach me, she saw that I was scared, I guess. She just led me back from the end of the lead rope and turned off the water. I could see that she was moving a little sore, but she laughed, "So baths are a 'no' I guess."

She put the hose on low and as I started to react again, she turned to me and just said, "Easy, momma I'm not going to try and do it that way again." I was still tense and placed myself at the very end of the *leadrope. She poured water into a bucket that she had brought and then turned it back off. She still had a hold of the line, but she was half turned and pouring some other stuff out of a bottle and into the bucket. She put a couple of rags into it, rang them nearly dry and with soft tension on the lead rope asked me over. I hesitated, but eventually I came near enough for her to touch me with the damp rag on one of the scrapes on my shoulder. I pulled away and she counter balanced against my weight. Not forcefully, but she definitely wasn't just going to let me go. I walked in a circle around her for maybe five minutes and then came to a stop, "Good girl, you're okay. That's a good girl." She approached me slowly and offered me a chunk of carrot from her pocket. I didn't even know she had carrots with her until that moment. I took it, whole mouthed, nearly took her hand with it- I hadn't eaten in a while and I was **hungry.** She attempted to clean my shoulder wound again and we repeated the pull back and circling for about three hours, every time I stopped circling around her she would give me a chunk of carrot. I think I have something like eight spots where I scraped myself up pretty good and we went through this routine for seven of them. By the last one I was standing, kind of, and she would give me a carrot every minute or so while I stood there. "See, there you go." She softly patted my neck and I relaxed into her hand and started to fall asleep when I heard her making an odd noise. I looked up and she was crying, her nose got all stuffy and she was making an odd breathing sound, but she just kept her hand where it was and continued to cry. "Thank you big girl. Thank you for giving me your trust for a moment." She let me loose and headed out of the pasture.*

These people (I'm trying my hardest not to call these ones monsters) are weird.

Chapter 11: The Trust Game

Do you remember when you were a child and you played the game of trust? Where everyone stood around in a circle. As the person in the middle you had to shut your eyes and fall back, trusting the people behind you to keep you from falling.
Every time we attach ourselves to a horse with a hard past, or really a horse of any type, we play this game.

Often times we feel like we are the ones in the middle, hoping we don't get dropped, that we are caught by the horse. The reality of the game we play is that the horse is ALWAYS in the middle. We are always on the outside circle hoping that the horse will trust us, hoping that it will allow us to guide it and keep it from falling. While we are the ones that are hoping to play the game, the horse stands in the middle with a quandry. Do I stand or do I trust?

August 13

I heard footsteps, but they were a little off and heavy, for a moment I looked up thinking it was Honey, but no. It was Denise, carrying a saddle and bridle and bucket full of grooming stuff all in one giant pile across her arms. I went from laying down to standing, fast enough that I think I pinched something in my hip. I was staring at her with what apparently was evident tension. She saw me out of the corner of her eye and laughed. "Oh don't worry old girl, it's not for you." She heaved the whole pile up onto the fence railing and headed for Blue's paddock.

The song she was singing yesterday kept playing in my head. She went and got Blue and tied him to the fence, as she groomed him she was humming to herself. Blue looked content, I enquired as to her behavior. "Why does she do that?"
Blue didn't even look at me, just continued to enjoy the moment. "Why does she do what? Don't tell me you have never been groomed."
I shook my head, "No. Not the grooming, why does she hum and sing?"
"Well, because we both enjoy it, I suppose. She has been doing that for as long as I have been here, and I assume for many years before that also. She wrote that song for us. Anytime I'm nervous, down or just not right, she seems to know and she sings that song."

Eventually Denise finished grooming, tacked Blue up and hand walked him for a few minutes, checking the cinch, checking that he was comfortable. She patted him on the neck and then mounted up. She was graceful and light as they rode around the paddock. I watched her very carefully, waiting for the pressure from the reins, the hard turn, the impact of what riders do. There was none, the reins stayed loose and low and I could barely pick up when she would cue him with her legs, there was almost no movement. They moved as a unit, not as though Blue was carrying her, but rather as though they were one thing. I had never seen riding like this, there was always pressure, there was always sore tongues and necks, spur marks, saddle pressure in the shoulders. This was very strange.

After a while she brought Blue next to the fence I was standing at and dismounted. I clenched and shut my eyes waiting for him to get hit. It seemed like I was waiting there for a long time- tense, prepared. After a about a minute I opened my eyes and they were both standing there, looking at me quizzically.

Denise took him over, tied and untacked Blue and resumed her humming. She brushed him and braided his mane, retrieved a carrot for him and turned him loose. He immediately went to the back corner of the paddock and rolled. Denise smiled and just watched him enjoy his after ride time. She grabbed the halter, hopped the fence, came to about 5 feet from me and waited. I looked over at Blue, he didn't seem in any discomfort, I looked at her and the halter. I walked away a little bit, but she just kept the same distance and followed along with me. When I stopped she stopped and stood, waiting again.

I didn't know what to expect or how this was going to go, but I signaled her that she could approach. She came over quietly and touched my shoulder. She just pet me for a while before putting the halter on me. She led me over and tied me to the fence, just as she had done with Blue. She hummed and brushed and checked my feet. She braided my mane and her soft touch reminded me of my owner's wife. She walked away for a moment and I prepared for the saddle, but it didn't come. She came back with a carrot and then just turned me loose. I am not understanding any of this. So I just stood there, kind of confused.

Denise looked at me with her head tilted a little bit, "Dear one, your days of rough riding and working are over. If one day you decide that you would like to ride, I would love to go for a ride on you. In the meantime, you are here for me to love and for Blue here to have a friend." She opened the gate that joined the two paddocks and Blue came trotting over to sniff me and investigate my paddock (as though his weren't identical). Blue looked up and beamed at me. I didn't know how to feel, but I thought that maybe I had finally found my home.

236's Journal

Nightmares. I hate the nightmares. They use to be only of the factory, but now there are so many layers. I was back at the kill pen, Taylor was walking through the pens looking at horses. She stopped at the pen I was in. She looked at all the horses and smiled at me, as I was walking over she pointed and said "that one." And the man who fed us there came to the gate with a gun, pointed it at me and fired, I heard a BANG!

I was awake instantly. Sweaty and breathing heavy and sore, it took me a minute to realize where I was, that I was sore because of the wounds from the other evening. I looked around frantically for a moment. I was looking for Grandma, but remembered that she wasn't there. I looked for Buck and he was lying a few feet away, a little harder to see in the dark, and for the fact that he sleeps like the dead. Today there were no people, except for the volunteer that comes around to feed us, he looked in on us and threw us hay, but nothing more. It was quiet.

As I began to eat, Buck came over tentatively. I think he was still feeling bad about kicking the snot out of me the other night. I decided that if horses play, I would try it with him. As he approached, I shied a little bit and feigned fear, "No, no!" I exclaimed, "Take all you want, just please don't kick me again!" He looked at me half irritated and half hurt, so I bumped him with my shoulder. "Thanks for taking care of me the other night old man, you saved my life."
He lit up. "You...you made a joke!" I smiled at him and we continued to eat, side by side. I don't ever think that I will be as close to him as I was with Grandma, but he is a good man to have around.

Buck's Journal

Honey made a joke! I am so proud of her. She is learning to be a horse. While it seems odd to me that a horse has to learn how to be a horse, she never really got the chance. She had never had a herd, or closeness or got to run and just be. I can't imagine what she went through, tied all day in a cramped stall, in a cramped barn with her babies taken away every time just to be put back into the barn and not be allowed to lay down, nonetheless just BE. What a horrible sadness.

Sometimes I think she makes up part of the story though, honestly who drinks horse urine? It doesn't even smell good, why would they actually put it in their bodies? That part never makes sense to me, there aren't

*any animals that go around drinking the pee of other animals. People
are strange and do weird stuff, but I still find that part very hard to
believe. On the other hand if it's not true then why did she spend her
life being tortured for the purpose of harvesting her urine.*

*I suppose my story seems just as strange to her. We are opposites in our
past, but identical in our loss. In spite of her past, she is trying and it's
so very difficult for her. Fourteen years old, she is just now learning to be
a horse and figure out who she is. I hope she finds herself and likes who
she is, who she is becoming. The rest of us are pretty fond of her.*

Sherry's journal
Honey has settled down and is beginning to adjust to life without
Lady. She is doing well with Taylor, although they definitely have
their rough patches. Taylor tries to play it off lighter than it
sometimes is. I'm pretty sure Taylor doesn't know that I watched
Honey drag her across the pasture, but I get it. I often get the, "She is
trying, but needs more time with this or that." I just smile and say
okay. Honey is a sanctuary horse now and Taylor seems to have taken
a real shine to her. They can play all they want, I trust Taylor with
Honey and I think that, though Honey struggles with it, that she
trust Taylor too-as much as she can.

August 20

I am beginning to relax here. Denise is kind and has shown nothing
but gentleness towards me and Blue. I am still unsure, and I still
tense when Denise goes to pet me, but maybe I'm okay. I guess to
some extent, I am simply too afraid to hope that something could be
this nice. That, of all the horses at the kill pen, somehow my life was

spared and I could be genuinely happy, with a person who is kind. Maybe this is all a dream and I will wake up tomorrow on a trailer to death, but I think for now, I will try to enjoy this dream.

236's Journal

I try, but no matter how hard I try I just can't bring myself to fully trust the monsters, I mean people. Taylor comes nearly every day, some days it takes us five minutes, some days it takes an hour for me to get to where I can allow her to get near me. I nearly always tense when she touches me, I just can't help it. Yesterday she tried to pick up my feet and I instinctively threw my leg out and ended up kicking her square in the chest. It knocked her back hard. I felt bad and I waited for her to get mad and hit me but she never did. She just took a minute to recover, came back to my shoulder and set a hand on me, "It's okay momma, we'll get there."

I don't know if we will ever get there. She tries to be patient with me and never shows anger or frustration, but I just don't know if I can ever really get there. She tried to pick up my front foot again and I tried to be strong and let her do it, but everything inside of me panicked. I bolted, tore the lead rope right out of her hand. She tried to calm me so that she could pick up the lead rope, it took a while, but she still didn't hit me. She stood next to me and looked at my legs and then looked at my face. "Okay momma, I am going to try something a little different." She pet my shoulder, and then she pet my shoulder and my leg to the knee, I tensed. She pet my shoulder to my knee again, and I still tensed. "There. I think that's a good first step," she gave me a chunk of carrot and limped out of my pasture, headed off to easier horses. I was disappointed with myself.

Buck came over and leaned into my shoulder, "You're doing good kid. You have come so far, and Taylor there adores you, she will give you all the time you need. You are having to learn to be a horse and to trust humans. That's a lot, even for a horse that already knows how to be a horse." He was trying to reassure me, and though I understood what he was saying to me, it was hard to think that I wasn't totally in control of my reactions.

August 21

It was too hot to do anything today other than try and stay cool. Blue splashed in his water a little bit and managed to get some on his chest, which almost immediately evaporated. He looked up at me with that mischievous smile and did it again, but this time he splashed me a little bit. He's a good horse and makes this transition in my life much easier. He doesn't seem to have a care in the world, and I often wonder what that is like, to be so free, to be so trusting. There is a large tree at the back end of our paddock that gives good shade in the evening. I walked over to it and stood there quietly for a while, just listening to the leaves rustle in the dry hot breeze. It at least sounded like it was cooling things down, even if it wasn't. Blue came over and leaned into me a little bit, but our body contact just made us both hot and sweaty nearly instantly, so he swayed back over a little bit.

I looked over at him and noticed he was staring up into the tree. So I followed his gaze. High on the top branches, worn and faded from the sunlight and exposure to many seasons, was a halter swaying gently with the movement of the tree. My eyes widened. I couldn't even fathom how it could have gotten up there, nonetheless *why* it was there. I looked back at Blue.

"He was the first." Blue said quietly. "He was long before my time. Momma told me about him, and the horse before us, had told her. And now I will tell you." Blue breathed deeply, and began his story. "Denise was young, 22 when she bought this ranch. And while for us 22 is older, for people it's very young. She loved horses and had always wanted one of her own. She went to breeders, and ranches and met a lot of very beautiful, well bred horses that would be glad to call her their owner; but she was looking for something different, she didn't even know what it was. One day she heard about a horse auction and decided to go see what was there. In a pen separated from all of the other horses was a nasty stallion, only 5 years old, but meaner than death. The man who owned the auction house saw her looking at that mean stud and told her that the stallion was unhandled, excessively mean and had killed the man that owned him. The story was that the man had tried to ride that stallion and the stud flipped over backwards and killed that man, then proceeded to kick and stomp the man afterwards. Denise looked at the stallion which was pacing and slamming into the sides of the pen. She asked the auction man how much the horse was. He told her that he was already purchased and that he couldn't disclose client information. She waited by that pen until the man that had bought him, a kill buyer, came to get him. She asked the man how much he paid for the horse and that she would like to buy it from him. The man laughed at her and told her that the horse would kill her and he was better off as meat on a table. Denise asked the man again, how much he had paid for the horse. 'Five hundred dollars, miss.' Denise offered him a thousand dollars for the horse.

The man criticized her. He told her that she could get a really nice horse at the auction for a thousand dollars. But Denise said that she didn't want a real nice horse, she wanted *that* horse. She told him that she would name the horse 'Hero'. The man laughed at her and brought the auction owner over as a witness, sold that stallion to Denise right there. Denise didn't even halter him, but guided him from behind onto the trailer to get him home. It took her two years before she could even get near that horse. And she worked with him almost every day. It took another three, working with him every day before she could ride him. She was the only person that he would let near him, he would straight attack anyone else that even tried to get close to the paddock.

She never once raised a hand in anger, she had five years of patience just to sit on that horse. Another two years before she could ride him out of this very paddock. When he was 15, they were out riding in the mountain trails and there was a mountain lion that came across the path. That horse spun to take off and Denise fell off of him. He got about twenty yards before he realized she was behind him. The lion launched at Denise and had his claws dug into her shoulder, you can still see the scarring across her chest and her back. That stallion turned around and fought that cat, they fought for a long time. The mountain lion tore that horse up pretty bad, but in the end Hero killed that cat. Denise was still on the ground, face down and bleeding badly. That stallion struck Denise and when she moved, he got ahold of the back of her belt and the back of her pants. Even though that horse was badly injured, he carried her out of the mountains.

Eventually some hikers saw the horse carrying the bleeding woman and tried to get close, but he wouldn't let them. He set Denise down gently and stomped the ground and backed away a little bit. The hikers came and checked the seemingly dead woman, terrified that she had been killed by her horse, but she was alive. They ran for the station house, where they trailers were parked and the rangers were. The horse picked Denise back up ever careful, and followed them all the way to the station. He put her back down and backed away when the rangers ran out to check her. They airlifted her out of there to the hospital, but there was still no one that could approach the badly injured horse. As soon as the helicopter headed out, that horse took off. They searched for him for days, but never found him.

When Denise was released from the hospital, she was heartbroken to find out that her horse was never found. Her truck and trailer were still at the trails and a friend had given her a ride home. There laying by the tree (Blue motioned to the tree in the grass where they get tied for bathing) was the horse that had saved her life. He had trekked, by himself, the 40 miles back home and laid in the yard to wait for her. She immediately called the vet, but his injuries were too bad and as she sat under that tree with that mean old horse's head on her lap, he went to run free in the skies.

She planted a tree for Hero, this tree, so that he could watch over all of the troubled horses that would need to be here after him. She has planted a tree for every horse that she has rescued since. There are five trees in that field including the one for my momma Stormy, the mare that raised me."

This woman really is a forever home. She knew I would be tough, but she was willing to give me all the time I need. I stared at the halter for a long time, until my neck ached. "Okay." It was all I could say.

236's Journal

It doesn't seem to matter how badly I mess up, Taylor still comes, takes her time and works with me. Today she came in and just brushed me, she checked my scrapes and sores, they are healing well. She spent time just brushing me, sometimes I would move or shy or twitch, but she just took her time and went slowly.

I still anticipate the punishment, but she is kind with me. I like the treats and I enjoy the company, but every time she goes to touch me, I get scared. It's like I can't totally control it, I just immediately panic. It's frustrating. I hope she knows I try.

Buck's Journal

I dreamt of my tribe. We were free, the sky was clear, it was spring. It was the day after the battle at the water hole, as though the death bird had never shown up. Sue was my main girl, she was always by my side. I loved her. She was a bay roan mare, she was 12 when she came to my herd. The other mares I had acquired through fighting with stallions, but not Sue- she left her stallion for me.

She was pregnant when we were rounded up. It was to be our first child together. We were separated in different pens after we were rounded up. She went into labor a few days after we arrived. I heard her call, over all of the commotion, over all of the noise...Congratulations Papa, your son is born. My son...who would never know the freedom from which we came. My son, who would never lead a tribe of his own.

*I dreamt last night that we **were** free. Me, Sue and my son grazing by the watering hole. My little boy, playing in the water without a care in the world. Young, feisty and full of life. It was a nice dream and often times, when this particular dream arises, I dread waking up. I lie in the grass for a long time, hoping that I can go back to sleep, hoping that I can go back to my dream, wishing I could go back. If he is even still alive, he is already old himself, 24 years. Forever one of the stories that will not be told, not be shared. But always a welcome dream. Perhaps, when I reach the sky range I will see my tribe again....and meet my son.*

Chapter 12: Loss

When we lose a horse, when we lose a friend or family, there is always that moment. I hope he/she knew...
I hope he knew that I loved him
I hope she knew that I tried
There is always a sense of loss and of unfinished business, even when we see it coming. Loss is part of life, it's what makes each day, each effort, each person- horse- pet- hope and dream, *precious*. There is always a hole left, in the shape of our loved ones. Memories that make us laugh and cry all at once because they are painfully real, and beautiful.
Unnecessary loss, unnecessary death is most painful.
We remember always, it is forever ingrained...the ones we couldn't save...that shouldn't have gone. They are the scars upon the heart of the driven. The wounds that bleed and feed the passion to save them all, though we know we can only save a few.

The lost are not forgotten.

August 21

I spent all night thinking of the story that Blue had told me. The patience of the woman and the horse that led to her passion for rescues. Blue and I talked long into the night about Denise and the type of person that she is. Blue has been here for ten years and I suppose if he says that she has always been kind to him, then I am ready.

I am ready to give my trust, to try harder to allow my life to change for the better. More than twenty years of my life spent with that harsh old man, I suppose that I can accept that some people are good. I still miss my family though, I miss Buck and Honey. I think about them every day, but it is getting less painful. This is to be my 5th home since May, just a few short months ago; but perhaps I can hope that this will be my last home. That one day I will have a tree with a halter hanging in it and never be forgotten by the heart of this woman.

236's Journal

They put five babies into the pasture next to us, the pasture that Buck lived in before he came to be part of my family. They were all about 4 months old. One of the volunteers set up buckets along the fence and filled them with what looked like milk. Buck was trotting the fence line with his one hitchy leg showing itself pretty plainly. He nickered at the little ones, I watched as he paced with anticipation, "Hello children!! Oh look at all of you, such beautiful babies. I just know you will all grow up to be so big and strong."

One of the little ones came over and Buck reached his head over the fence as far as he could to nuzzle the fuzzy little beast, a filly. She giggled and asked him about this place. She is a very serious little thing. She is what I imagine Grandma looked like as a baby, rich bay and fluffy. I smiled a little bit. The little girl was asking Buck if he knew where their mothers were, and he said no. But assured the little child that he would look out for all of the children. The little girl was spunky, "Well mister, I can look out for myself, thank you very much!"

Buck grinned widely at her, but you could still see the little bit of sadness behind his eyes. He spent all day at that fence, running and playing and bucking up like he was still a five year old range stud. It was actually quite beautiful to watch. I sat back a little bit so that I could take in the whole scene and as I watched Buck and the babies playing along the fenceline I couldn't help but wonder if maybe, by just a sliver of chance, if one of my babies had survived and was out there somewhere.

Buck's Journal

New babies! There are five new foals in the pasture next to us and each one of them is just so beautiful. There are four nurse mare foals and then there's the little ornery bay filly. Her name is Tundra, and she is a mustang. I noticed the way she smells before I noticed the brand on her neck. Why do they cold fire such little ones? She is smaller than the others but built for the rugged country, she must be from one of the mountain tribes. She's a fiery one. Their arrival sent me daydreaming again. Jenna, one of the mares in my tribe, had given me a little bay filly, much similar to this one- strong, fierce, brave and feisty. We had named her Blaze, because that filly caused havoc in the whole tribe and

was lightening quick. We would laugh as she would use the rest of the
herd as her personal obstacle course. Babies are beautiful.
The orphan foals, the nurse mare foals are different. They have never
known real freedom. They were with their mommas, likely in stalls,
and then they were orphans and sold to a kill pen, to await vicious end
to their short lives. I looked up for a little while and looked at all the
horses here at the rescue. We are all byproducts of humanity.

August 23

I woke up this morning, ready. Ready to belong, ready to be loved. I
waited at the gate for Denise, Blue standing next to me. We waited.
But Denise didn't come, around 8am a car pulled into the driveway
and a woman neither of us knew, got out. She went to the barn and
got our hay. This was very odd. She filled our waters and looked us
over for a moment. This unknown woman then got in the car and
left. "Blue! Who was that? Where is Denise?" He looked up at me
with a touch of worry across his face.
"I really don't know." This can't be right. Where is our person? We
waited for her all day, but she never came. The woman in the car was
back in the evening and went through the same routine, feed, water,
look us over and leave. I became very uncomfortable.

236's Journal

The babies next door have brought out a new life in Buck. He is playing
and chasing and being generally goofy. The children race him and kick
up and laugh and have a wonderful time playing with the old man
through the fence. I was standing in the shade, near the fence line when
one of the little buggers snuck up on me and kicked at the fence, bout

scared me out of my skin. I jumped and turned to see Tundra running off laughing hysterically at herself. I just laughed, "Come here you little beast! I'll getcha!" I stomped and snorted with the best scary Auntie move I could muster. She thought it was hilarious and continued on with her escapades. I stomped and hollered and when one of the babies would come to the fence and kick up at me I would pretend that they startled me which they just thought was the funniest thing.

My mind momentarily wandered to Grandma, I hope she is doing okay in her new life, I hope she is alive and well. I miss her dearly.

Buck's Journal

*Ah, babies. I love those little buggers. All joy and playful, sometimes it feels like I am back with my herd. There is a life in foals that barn horses forget after a time. Like every horse is born a mustang, but some of them forget- they lose the play, life becomes serious. I often take it upon myself to remind both horses and people, that life is **alive**, dynamic, fun. There is sorrow, but that doesn't have to keep you from living.*

Honey actually played today, the little filly Tundra has taken it upon herself to teach Honey how to horse. It's beautiful. Tundra is a vibrant young filly, but there is a fire in her that I just love to watch. These babies make domestic life a little easier.

Sherry's Journal
Buck has been great for Honey. I sat on the porch and drank my coffee and watched as buck played with the foals we turned out in the

pasture next to them. That boy does love his babies. As I watched this beautiful morning unfold, I saw Honey stomp and PLAY! I have not seen that mare be anything but terrified or stoic since she got here, but she was actually playing a little bit. She is becoming a horse and I couldn't be more pleased to be witness to some of the horse's greatest attributes, forgiveness and adaptability. Humans would not bounce back so easily from what this poor mare has endured for the majority of her life and I was honored to be a party to her healing.

August 24

Denise is still missing. Blue and I are beginning to get scared. Neither of us know what is going on, the woman in the car was back again today feeding, watering. We spent most of the day watching the driveway, calling from time to time, but to no avail.
I finally broke the silence, "Blue. Do you think they sent her to slaughter? What are we going to do if she never comes back? Will we have to go back to the rescue? Will we just stay here with the weird lady? What do you think is going on?" Blue looked at me and just shook his head. He had all the same questions and none of the answers. Neither of us ate this evening.

About 1 am a car pulled into the driveway, Blue and I ran to the far side of the paddock, we know the sound of familiar cars, and neither of us knew this one. It came to a stop in front of the house and the silhouette of a person was lit up from the porch light. We couldn't see who it was, but after the car left we heard the person quietly call. "Where are you my babies?"

It was Denise! She was home! We both ran to the fence and nickered and chattered and huffed. She stood with us in the dark for a little while just petting and loving and getting affectionately mauled by Blue and myself. "Well!" She laughed. "I'm glad to see you both missed me. I missed you too, my lovelies. I'm sorry I had to leave for a while. My mother has been sick and it was time for her to leave this earth. I had to be there with her." She brought us carrots and told us that she would see us in the morning, headed into the house. Blue and I proceeded to eat the meal we had left, and slept soundly knowing our person was safely home.

236's Journal

Taylor says that I am making progress, honestly I think she just says that on days where she can leave without injury. I don't mean to hurt her, but I get nervous or scared or react before I even realize I have done it. I am still very tense for about the first half an hour after she catches me, though the catching part only takes us 5-10 minutes now. She runs her hand along my legs and most days that's okay, some days I run in a circle around her, some days I tear out of her hand or inadvertently end up kicking her, or stomping a foot. I try so hard, I try to trust her I try to be a horse, I try to do the things that I see the other horses enjoy, but I just don't know if I will ever get there. I have never known these things. I have never had a bath, or smelled like soap. I have never had someone mess with my legs and feet- at the factory they just wait until the long part of the hoof broke off. I had never been pet or brushed, or given carrots, or even laid down to rest. This is all still so new to me. I feel like a baby, but even the babies are progressing faster than I am. It is frustrating. Taylor says that I am one of the horses of her heart. I am not sure what that means. I like her I really do, but I am still not sure what it all means.

Buck is sleeping hard. I think the babies wear him out, though I know he loves it. He was dreaming earlier, I think that he was dreaming of his herd, I heard him sigh the name "Sue" and then he smiled a little bit. Right now he's just still, resting peacefully. I am up at night often and I watch him, even now I cannot sleep so soundly through the night. Perhaps it's something else I will learn to do here. It's late though and the sun will be up soon. I suppose I should rest for a little while. I must say I do love that I can lay down and stretch out, even if I have not come to sleep peacefully quite yet.

August 25

Denise came out early today, she had tack, a saddle and grooming stuff all piled in her arms again. I breathed deeply, looked at the grand old tree at the end of our paddock-Hero's tree, and then trotted over to meet her at the fence. I was so excited to be the new me that I almost knocked all the stuff out of her hands. I hadn't meant to and I shied a little after bumping her.

"Oh, well hello my love!" She giggled excitedly and didn't even bother to pile the stuff carefully on the fence. She just dumped the whole pile on the ground, came over and hugged me around the neck. At first I thought it was going to get violent, but then I relaxed into her arms and we just stood there for a long time. It was nice, I had never felt such warmth from a person. Even my owner's wife was kind to me, but never so passionate about her kindness. When she let go she just looked at me and stroked my face, quite gently, smiling. I looked over and nudged the saddle to let her know that if she wanted to, I was ready to be hers.

She looked at the saddle and then looked at me, "Are you sure?" I nudged it again and looked around at my back to make my intentions clear. "Well, okay but let's start small, since we are both new with one another. I'll be right back." She beamed at me and then headed off back to the barn, after a few minutes she returned with what looked like a saddle pad that had a cinch attached to it. I had never seen one of these contraptions before. I looked over at Blue, while Denise was headed back to us.

"It's a bareback pad," he assured me. "They are really comfortable on your back, it works just like a saddle, but you can feel the rider. It's soft and not heavy."

Denise came back, tied me to the fence and began to sing, "You are the beauty of my soul. My heart attached to the end of the rope. Hoofbeats for heart beats, you are part of me. My soul, my mare, the loveliest dream. Lovely. Lady. The horses I save that save me. You are the beauty of my soul. My heart attached to the end of the rope..." She sang as she groomed me. A song...just for me? It was the most beautiful thing I had ever heard.

She placed the bareback pad on me, cinched it up, but not very tight and began to walk me around the paddock. It was odd, it didn't feel like I actually had anything on my back and I kept looking back to make sure it was still there. "What do you think, my love?" Denise enquired. I nuzzled her for a moment and she brought me back to the fence. She put reins on my halter and gently slid over onto my back from the top rail of the fence. I tensed ever so slightly, ready for the kick to go. "There is no rush, love." She just sat on me for a long time, we didn't go anywhere, she just stroked my mane and my neck until there was no tension at all. She picked up the reins and just clicked. There was no pressure on my face, which I was not accustomed to, she clicked again and I took a tentative step forward.

We walked around the paddock, I caught on quickly that she would move her hips just a little to the direction we were going and I began to follow the cues. It was the softest rider that I have ever carried. After about 15 minutes she leaned back a little bit and I stopped. She got off and her arms came up, which I automatically assumed was going to be a fist and kind of braced, closing my eyes. When I opened my eyes she was standing there next to me, arms open a little bit. I leaned my head into her chest and she hugged me. This was nice.

236's Journal

When I got up this morning, Buck was still sleeping. I went and got a drink of water and looked over to him, watching him sleep. It took me a moment to realize something was off. Buck was in the same position that he had been when I laid down, he hadn't moved even a leg. I went over to him carefully, slowly and put my nose down by his nose, but I couldn't feel him breathing. I used a front foot and bumped him gently, there was no reaction. NO! I bumped him again and checked his face with my nose...he was cold.

I wailed...loud. The sun was barely up but I think I woke the whole farm. It was not a normal sound, it was all the pain and loneliness inside of me welling up and exiting my soul, not just my lungs. It was anguish. Taylor was already at the ranch, she was out in the arena working with another horse when she heard me. She looked up and called a volunteer over to take the horse she was working with. She and Sherry were headed my way in moments. I was still crying when they got there.

They got to the gate and saw me standing over Buck. They both came in and slowly approached. I backed up a few steps to allow them space to check my friend. Deep down inside I still hoped that he was alive, but I knew better. They checked him and talked for a while, then Taylor stayed and Sherry left. Taylor came over to me, "I'm so sorry momma." She stroked my neck while I stood, just staring at one more friend... gone. I am lonely and sad, but I am also happy for Buck. He is finally home and free again with his herd on the sky range.

Taylor put a lead rope on me and took me out, led me down the aisles past other horses, many of those horses asking what happened, but I couldn't answer. I was alone again and I didn't know what was going to happen to me. Taylor put me in a stall and went to talk to Sherry. They spoke for a long time, after which Taylor headed back to me and Sherry headed off in another direction. Taylor climbed up onto the railing of my stall and just sat there with me for a long time. It wasn't an awkward silence, more of a mutual respect and quietness, a stillness.

I saw a truck and trailer go by and head down the aisles of horses. After a while it came back by and I saw it pull over to a field, where there were rose bushes. It parked and I saw Joe go by on a tractor. He pulled up next to the truck. Got out and talked to the driver, who I assumed to be Sherry and then began to dig a hole, long and deep. When he was done digging the hole he left for a while, coming back with a tiny rose bush, which he placed gently on the ground. The driver of the truck pulled around and backed the trailer up to where the hole was and they pulled my friend out and gently as possible slid him into the hole. Joe took the tractor and filled the hole in. They looked over at me and Taylor. "I'll be right back, momma."

Taylor jumped down off the railing and headed over to join the other two people. They stood there for a long time and then Joe grabbed a shovel from near the trailer and dug a small hole, Sherry placed the little rose bush in the hole and Taylor proceeded to fill in the dirt carefully around the root base. They stood there for a long time in silence, and I could see that all three of them were crying, they were **mourning**. *I realized in that moment that Buck was not special only to me. I also realized that the rose garden was huge. It was a place of memories and souls never forgotten.*

I am the wary mare, and I am alone.

Sherry's Journal

Today was heartbreaking. Buck passed quietly, but he has been a staple here for more than 20 years, he was one of the first horses that we took in. It feels like a part of me is missing. He is back with his herd now, but I am totally wrecked over his passing. We buried him in the rose garden and marked his grave with a yellow rose. He will forever be the only yellow rose in the garden. Every resident we lose has a rose in the garden, but Buck I thought would outlive us all. Tomorrow I go to do a home visit with Denise and Lady. Denise has informed me that Lady has really settled in nicely, so perhaps it will pull me out of this funk.

August 27

It was cooler this afternoon, there was a breeze. I can feel that the
season will change soon to when the tree begin to shed their leaves.
Denise came out with her arms full of tack, apparently she doesn't
believe in making two trips. My heart is happy here are we are
beginning to form a family.

Denise tied both Blue and I to the fence and groomed us while
humming, as per usual. She saddled Blue and put the bareback pad
on me. We were going on an outing. Blue says there is a trail about a
mile down the road. They often ride down to the trail and spend
about 2 hours riding out in the woods. It sounded pleasant enough.

Denise mounted Blue, tied my lead line to the saddle horn and off we
went. There were cars that would slow down and take a wide berth
around us, giving us plenty of room on our trip. Denise would wave
and holler a thank you or just nod in their general direction. We were
just cruising along, joyously.

There was a truck coming up behind us, as many had done so far.
This one didn't slow down, instead it kept speeding down the road
and I could hear the music getting louder. As it approached I heard
laughter and they laid on the horn, one of the young people that was
in the back of the truck yelled and banged on the side of the truck
while the other passengers roared with laughter, as they came up
nearly behind us. It all happened so fast.

Blue startled and reared, as Denise tried to get him under control.
The tension on the lead line pulled me forward and I ricocheted off

the side of the truck, pulling Denise and Blue directly into the path of the truck as I bounced off and spun. Blue was hit by the front corner and the headlight shattered. The truck spun but Denise came off Blue and there was just chaos. The truck hit something and then spun out into the ditch along the side of the road. Blue was lying on the ground, injured badly, he couldn't get up. I was bleeding from my shoulder and was having trouble breathing, but was still tied to Blue.

I searched frantically but I could not see Denise. Then I saw her, she had fallen between Blue and the truck when it caused Blue to spook, it looked like she got run over by the back tire as it spun past us. She wasn't dead, but she was very badly injured. She was breathing, but not really moving.

The car coming from the other direction had seen the whole thing and stopped. The woman was on her phone and talking frantically to the person on the other end. She was moving fast straight for Denise. "No-No-No!" I heard her screaming. I was panicked, and was dancing around, trying not to step on Blue, when I realized it was Sherry! She had come to do a home check, I remembered Denise had mentioned that yesterday, that Sherry was going to be coming by today.

After checking on Denise, she came over and untied me from Blue's saddle. Took me over to a nearby tree and tied me there, took my saddle pad off and headed back to the chaos. Blue was bleeding badly and couldn't get up, he kept trying and collapsing back onto the ground. Then I heard sirens and there were people everywhere. There were about five people over working on Denise. They got her situated and loaded her very carefully onto a rolling bed, that they loaded into a van with lights. They took off with sirens screaming. The vet showed up and sedated Blue and myself, just enough to make me calm. I watched as they used giant loud scissors to cut part of the truck away. There were four people in the cab, the driver was bloody and they carefully took him out. He had some sort of brace around his neck and they put him on a rolling bed, into another van and that one also took off with sirens blaring. The medical people were talking into the truck, one of the medics climbed in and they were able to get one of the boys out and onto a stretcher. The other two boys they were a little less careful with, and they took them out in big bags. All because they thought it would be funny to go to fast and scare a horse. Three lives lost in a matter of seconds.

The vet and Sherry were bent over Blue, they were checking him and I overheard the vet say that he was sorry. Blue had shattered his pelvis when the truck hit him and was bleeding on the inside from a ruptured something. The vet went back to his truck, drew up two large syringes of stuff and went back to Blue. Blue stretched his head out and found me, We just stared at each other while Sherry held Blue's head in her lap and the vet sent him off to the sky range.

There on the side of the road three lives lost, with three more still unknown. All because they thought it was fun to scare a horse. He was only 11. I was finally home. Everything! Everything has been stripped from me in just a few seconds.
Now what?

Sherry and the vet came over to me and checked my shoulder. He said he didn't know if it was broken, but he would have to take x-rays and at the very least get me stitched up. Sherry stayed with me as Joe showed up with a trailer; a second trailer, driven by Taylor was not far behind. They loaded me onto the trailer that Taylor was driving. Taylor got out and spoke with Sherry about what happened. When she saw Blue laying there shattered, she began to sob, horribly, uncontrollably. I heard Sherry tell Taylor to take me back to the ranch, that the vet was going to meet us there and get x-rays of my shoulder. My heart broke as we drove away, I didn't know if they knew about the trees...

Sherry's Journal

Today was the worst day I have ever had. I have been at the hospital all night waiting for news of Denise. She is still in surgery. It was just a disaster. I tried calling the ranch to get an update on Lady but have not heard anything back. I will keep trying. I keep playing the scene back through my mind, God was a horrific scene it was, it still is. I have talked to the police three times about what happened. This was all so unnecessary. Why can't people slow down? Why do they think it's funny to risk the lives of horses and other people. I just don't understand this. I just don't understand.

Chapter 13: The Great Mourning

Those who think it funny to speed past horses and their riders are often oblivious to the dangers that they can cause. Lives can be lost in the blink of an eye. Damage and injury can ensue. The animals that we are riding, entrust us with their lives, and we entrust them with ours. When you see a horse and rider on the road, please for the sake of their safety and yours, slow down or stop. While some animals are fine with traffic, some are new to it. Scaring a horse for the purpose of entertainment can become a horribly tragic situation so very quickly. These animals mean everything to us and it is simply not worth costing them their futures or yours.

When tragedy strikes, the world shifts. Often, things happen that we don't understand and overcoming those obstacles are typically the hardest mountains that we have to climb.

236's Journal

I was still mourning Buck when Taylor and Joe both took trucks and trailers and went tearing out of the ranch. They looked panicked. Momentary chaos in what was a silent and sorrowful evening. I didn't touch my hay, I just stood in my stall with my head down. Occasionally I would look out to the rose garden, and the tiny little bush that now represents such a mighty horse.

After about an hour the vet pulled in and started getting set up for something. I heard the crunch of gravel and saw Taylor pulling in very slowly with the trailer. She was crying when she got out, her face was red and her eyes were swollen. She went around to the back and took a horse out of the trailer and directly into quarantine, where the vet was. I didn't see the horse, but I guess it was in a bad way because Taylor was covered in blood and I kept seeing her run back and forth from the Vet's truck fetching things for him. I don't know what was going on, but it was a temporary distraction from the death of the morning.

After about another hour Joe came back with his trailer and parked it, he was covered in sweat and blood. He headed straight for the quarantine barn. After a few minutes I heard a noise from the barn. It was a soft nicker. My head snapped towards quarantine and my ears perked up. No!

I called as loudly as I could and began to pace ferociously in my stall. I called again and waited. It was faint, and a little broken, but it was her. Grandma! My mind spun! Why was everyone covered in blood?! Is she hurt? Oh no, not her too. Not Grandma and Buck! This can't be happening.

*Taylor made her way over to me, she looked exhausted. I was pacing
and calling and fussing and she still managed to come to me gently.
"Easy, Momma." She took the halter from the rail and I brought my
head down for her to fasten it. As soon as she opened the stall door, I
was pulling her across the 30 yards to the Quarantine barn. "Easy,
Honey, easy..." She gave a little tug on the lead rope and I slowed down
a touch, but was kind of half trotting/half walking at a really slow
pace. She brought me in and put me in the stall next to Grandma.
"Take it easy with the old girl, Honey. She has had a rough go of things
today too."*

*Taylor headed over to help the vet clean up the mess that had been
created in the barn. Grandma was heavily sedated and her head hung
very low, her lips half open and she didn't look like she was even aware
of what was going on around her. She was scraped up badly and had
stitches across her side from her withers all the way down and around
in a wide half circle on her shoulder.*

*The vet was talking to Joe and Taylor, he asked where Sherry was and
Joe said that she had gone to the hospital to stay with Denise, who was
in surgery. The vet started talking about Grandma. "She broke her
scapula, tore the nucha, trapezius and deltoid, she has two broken ribs
and is scraped up besides. She's one tough horse! Honestly I don't know
if she is going to make it, it's going to be a long time on stall rest and a
long road of rehab for her. I gave her fluids, got the bleeding stopped,
reattached the major tears and gave her some iv antibiotics. The break
in her scapula isn't huge, but she is going to have to take it really easy
and stay calm." He gave them a couple of tubes of what looked like
wormer, but it was blue- they called it dorm or derm or something. He
also gave them a bottle of tablets and told them that he would be back*

in the morning, unless something happened and that they could call
him any time if there was a problem.
What the hell happened?

August 26

I still keep hoping that I will wake up; hoping that this is all a bad
dream. My shoulder and my head are pounding. I am back in
quarantine, at the rescue. Honey is next to me. For a moment I
thought maybe the whole last month had been a dream and that we
had just arrived here from the kill pen. I was confused and didn't
really register all that was going on. But then I tried to move and my
shoulder rang out in vicious pain.

I heard a faint whisper, "Grandma?" Honey sounded as if she had
been crying. Her voice was a little raspy and had an edge to it.
"Grandma, are you okay? What happened?" I couldn't speak, I could
barely think. I didn't know if Denise was dead or alive. I pictured
Blue there on the side of the road. My heart was overwhelmed with
emotion.
"I..." I choked up, took a deep breath, but was still too full of
emotion to speak entirely clearly. "I don't know what happened. We
were riding...and then the truck...I just...I don't know what
happened." It was all I could do to get that much out.

Taylor had slept in the barn with us and checked on me throughout
the night. Currently she was asleep on a couple of hay bales, using
her jacket as a makeshift blanket. I was watching her, when Sherry
came in. Sherry searched and saw Taylor, went over to her quietly
and put a hand on her shoulder. Taylor was suddenly up and wide

awake. She wasn't even fully standing before she started giving a report about my condition. Her words were all running together, "Doc said broken shoulder, tears, we have meds and..."

Sherry stopped her. "It's okay. Okay. Breathe, take a minute. I brought you coffee. It's been a long and rough day for everyone, let's just sit for a little while." They sat there on the hay bales for a long time, sipping their coffee and not speaking. Sherry looked exhausted and was still covered in blood and dirt, wearing the clothes she had on yesterday. I don't know if Sherry knows that she holds the human herd together, like a lead mare caring for her clan.

Taylor took a breath, and with two hands grasping the cup, sipped at her coffee. She started, "She going to be okay, but she is going to need a long lay up." Taylor started telling her about the surgery, the break and the tears. I saw Mac in my mind, being loaded onto the slaughter truck, with his break and his tear. I let out an involuntary low moan, not from the physical pain, but from the emotions I was trying not to let well up and out. Taylor got up, "Okay Lady. I got you." She crushed up a pill into some grain and gave it to me. Taylor looked over her shoulder to Sherry, "Denise?" I was watching....waiting.

Sherry set her coffee down, shook her head, "She was run over by the back tire of the truck, after she fell. She broke her hip, her right arm and a bunch of ribs. She had some internal bleeding that they were able to get under control, they think. She is in ICU. They don't know if she is going to make it or not, it's very touch and go right now. I'll head back out to the hospital this afternoon. After a shower and a change of clothes."

Denise was alive, not well, but for the time being- alive.

236's Journal

I don't even think Grandma really noticed that I was here. I mean, she noticed but something bad has happened. Her person has a bunch of stuff going on and might die. From the way she looks, Grandma almost died. They kept us both up throughout the day and through tonight. Taylor finally left when she saw that Grandma was doing okay. Before she headed out of the barn, Taylor came over to my stall and I backed away a little bit, "Take good care of her Honey, she has had the worst day of all of us I think." Sherry put a bunch of shavings into Grandma's stall and it made the whole barn smell like trees.

She came over and spent some time just standing next to my stall, "How are you holding up big girl? I know there has been a lot of stuff going on today, I just wanted to check on you before I head to bed. It's been a rough one for everyone, but you my stoic friend tend to hide behind your strength. We are here for you too, sweetheart." It was late and sleep sounded just right, maybe I would wake up from this nightmare.

Sherry's Journal
What a long and horrendous couple of days. Taylor and Joe, what would I ever do without them. I was able to stay at the hospital until Denise was out of surgery and somewhat stable. She was still asleep when I left, but stable-ish. I finally got ahold of Joe long enough for him to tell me that Lady was still being looked after by the vet. Taylor stayed with Lady all through the night, giving her bute, making sure

that she was doing okay. That girl is a life saver. I honestly don't know what I would do without her and Joe.

August 27

It was a long night and lying down hurt, I couldn't seem to find a comfortable place or position so I spent most of the night standing up and taking short naps. The scene on the road kept playing through my mind. It was the laughter that bothered me the most. There was laughter and then there was death.

Denise is badly hurt, Blue is gone, two people from the truck are gone. Just laughter and then death. Every time I shut my eyes I could see Dense lying on the ground, Blue lying on the ground. It was all too much to process and I felt lost. I don't think I will ever understand what was funny to the people in the truck.

236's Journal

Grandma was silent through all of today, occasionally I would hear her choke up, trying to hold back tears. I am trying to give her time to process, but I can see that even more than the pain in her body, there is a deeper, more real pain that she is trying to cope with.

All I can do is be here for her. Sherry, Joe and Taylor came through regularly and checked on us both. I haven't yet told her about Buck. I'm not sure she needs to hear it right now. When the time comes, we will lean on each other as we have done so many times over the past few months. For now I will be her ever present sentry.

August 28

Sherry came in today and gave me my pill in some grain. After about a half and hour she came back with Taylor and they moved me and Honey to the larger stalls outside. As Sherry began to take my halter off she leaned in very close to me. "They moved Denise this morning, Lady. I don't know how long it will be, but she is as tough as you are, she is going to make it. I think you understand, I hope you understand," she stroked my neck gently. I silently considered the information for a long time.

Honey stayed quiet mostly. From time to time she would nicker and gently nuzzle me over the fence. Something must have happened to Buck, she didn't say it but when she looks at me there is something unsaid in her eyes. I was grateful for her silence, I am not sure that I am yet prepared to ask the question.

Sherry's Journal
I went to visit Denise at the hospital early this morning. I have been there nearly every day. She was awake when I arrived, but still on heavy pain medication. I let her know that Lady was doing okay but that she too had recuperation time. She asked if Blue had made it and I had to break her heart all over again.I tried to give her information without being overly detailed about the nature of his injuries. When I got back to the ranch, we moved Lady and Honey to the bigger 20x20 stalls outside. When I led Lady into her stall I told her about Denise. I don't know if I am stupid, foolish or what, but I am convinced that she understands. I hope she understands.

August 29

I am beginning to feel a little better today. My body still hurts like the dickens, but my mind and heart I suppose are beginning to heal a little bit. I apologized to Honey for being so distracted. She reached over the rails and nuzzled me. "It's okay Grandma, I know something bad happened, and you don't have to talk about it. I'm just glad you are mostly okay. When you are ready, if you are ever ready, I am here for you." Honey is such a sweet friend. In the midst of her own heartbreak (she tries to hide her pain, but it is written on her face) she was my comforter.

I spent the day telling her stories. Rather than spilling my pain once again, I told Honey about Denise, her sweet nature, how she made songs special for each of her horses. I told her about Blue, that he was a PMU foal from her same facility. Her eyes glimmered ever so slightly at that news. I explained that he was the foal of a mare she had been transported with. "Then there is a small hope." She said. "His very existence says that there is a small hope that some of my 12 children are alive. There is the possibility that they were rescued." She nodded her head, a glimmer of hope renewed in her scorched heart. I continued to tell her my stories. It made me think of Buck, when we gathered around and shared stories of our past, of beauty, of life.

I told her about the trees in the back field, but for some reason didn't tell her about Hero and his tree. At the mention of the trees, I saw her eyes flick to the rose garden and she smiled, it was a smile tainted with sorrow. "Buck." she motioned towards the tiny rose bush in the garden, towards the end of one of the rows. It was newly planted.

I nuzzled her. "I'm sorry that I was not here for you my friend."
She looked at me and smiled a little. "I got to be here for Buck. Just
like he was here for me the night they took you away. It was supposed
to be this way- he helped me a lot. I played with baby horses and
learned more about being a horse. You were learning to trust from
your person and new friend Blue, I was learning to trust from Buck.
Both of us had growth that needed to happen. Parts of our present
that needed to impact our futures. While I hate that it happened, I
am glad that we both learned and had a friend to help us. And now
we help each other. Is your person going to be okay?"

I was shocked. Not because Honey was concerned for the welfare of
my person, Honey is kind and sweet. I was shocked because it was the
first time I had heard her NOT call them monsters. She had grown
and come into her own, in our time apart. I stared at her for a
moment and realized that there was no spite or anger in my friend
any longer, only sorrow. I told her that eventually yes, my person
would be okay.

236 Journal

*A lot of healing was done today I think. Grandma and I bonded over
pain and loss, much as we had the first few days that we had known
each other. The difference is that this time there was less confusion, less
fear of violent death; we knew that **these** people were trying to help us.
Grandma and I shared stories throughout the day, she told me of her
person and her friend Blue. I shared stories of Buck and his crazy antics
with the children in the adjoining pasture.
It was nice to have my friend back, though I was trying to accept that
some day her person would be back for her. I didn't know what my*

future held, but I knew that Grandma would be okay and that was enough for me now.

September 1

We have spent many days in these stalls. From time to time Taylor comes around and hand walks Honey for about a half an hour to an hour. Then working with her in the stall, trying to continue to earn her trust. She is always gentle and kind to my friend. I watched today as Taylor worked with Honey on picking up her feet.

Honey would tense and clench her jaw, trying to comply and then close her eyes and pick her foot up and slam it back down to the ground. Taylor was tireless in her efforts to make a friend of Honey. This woman understood that Honey was trying, complying as best she could. After a long time and lots of tries, Honey picked up her foot and suspended it in the air for a moment, then brought back down and backed away from Taylor a step. Taylor smiled at her, "That was amazing! Good job Momma!" There was no defeat in Taylor, only praise and kindness. It was nice to see that someone had dedicated themself to Honey, as Denise had done for me.
When Taylor put her back in the stall, Honey looked at me with concern. "I try so hard, but I just can't get it, I can't convince myself that I'm not going to be hurt. I know it, but I should get it by now."

I smiled at my conflicted friend. "Honey, dear one, you are trying. Taylor is happy to help you try. She knows that you have a lot to overcome, and she is simply happy to help you try. We all are."
Honey stretched and then flopped herself onto the ground, tucking her feet up underneath her. For a large animal she could become

quite small and innocent. There was still a lot of frustration in her, but she knows she is loved and I think to a point she just enjoys the simple fact that she *can* lay down. It was quite amazing to me, we were only gone from each other for a little while, but our bond has rekindled stronger than before. I stood over my friend as best I could while she slept, keeping vigil through the evening.

Chapter 14: Change

Change is imminent. There are times when our lives change for the better and times when life changes for worse. But even when life seems stagnant, there is change. Small changes in the world around us create changes to our little personal world.

Being part of change is a choice that we make, it's an effort we put in to something greater than ourselves. I urge you to be a part of making a change. Stop for the horse and rider on the road. Speak against cruel slaughter practices, against the violence that takes place in the round up of our wild horses.
Volunteer or donate to your local rescues. Adopt. Write. Call. Be Change.

If you are one that thinks you cannot make a difference, it only takes one-you. There is such a huge trickle effect, such a huge difference that your one move, your one change makes, sometimes you cannot always see it, but it can change the lives of many- your one small choice.
Be a voice for change, be a part of it.

September 2

The vet was out today to check on my progress. I suppose I am doing okay. I hurt but mostly I am just sad. I was just getting to know my family. He says I am healing the way I should be, at least physically. It will still be a long time before they allow me back out in a pasture. I don't know if I will ever get to go back home to my person.

At least I have Honey, and her presence, watching her and Taylor together warms my heart. Even though Taylor doesn't own her, I think Taylor is her person. They struggle together, but Taylor is the only one who really tries with Honey. She is the only person who has given Honey a chance to try. I don't know if Honey will ever make it to really trusting anyone, but Taylor is certainly working with her towards it.

I, on the other hand, sit here- and think. Today I was thinking about my home before, with the mean old man. What a difference between that home and the one that I just lost. My old home was all business, there was no scratches or petting or carrots (unless his wife snuck them to me). You know you did a good job because you didn't get walloped and you were elite if you got a pat on the neck from time to time, but there was nothing intimate and touch was rare. The differences between him and Denise were stark. Denise was intimate always, touch was a regular occurrence and dare I say more important to her than it was to Blue and myself. It was about relationships, not business. It was all pretty amazing. I hope she is healing well. She was my person, and dare I hope, can be my person again one day.

I adore Taylor, but I swear that woman is crazy. Today we worked on "feet and fly spray" as she called it. That nutcase tried to spray me with this god awful smelling stuff that I am pretty sure is going to kill me. We started off with me, once again, trying to pick up my feet. I stomped her foot once, I tried to run away twice, I was able to pick it up twice without total panic, and then we worked on the other front leg. I get frustrated, and sometimes I feel worthless, but she always encourages me, and praises me for trying even when I mess up. Taylor keeps joking saying that if we both survive to see me pick up the fronts, maybe we will start working with the back legs. Crazy woman. I don't want to kill her, but those back legs are how I defend myself and I am just not sure what would happen if she got back there.

Then she brought out this bottle of stuff and it shot liquid at me while it made a weird hissing sound and I totally freaked out. I reacted to the sound, the fact that she was pointing it at me, the feeling like she had just shot little bugs onto my hair. It was worse than the water. Nope! I hit the end of the lead rope and walked quickly in a circle around her with as much tension and space between us as I could. She held on, and stopped spraying, but I kept walking. It was about ten minutes before I settled down enough to stop. She came over gave me piece of carrot and then tried to spray me again. I took off on the end of the line in a circle again. We continued this routine for about an hour before I realized that she wasn't even spraying it at me, she was spraying it at the ground. I stopped and processed that for a minute. She repeated the carrot and praise. She backed up and sprayed it at the ground and rather than pull away I just tensed, but was able to fight the urge to flee. She praised me and led me back to the stall. "Good job momma, that's a hard one to get through. You did good." She stroked my neck and shoulder for a few minutes, giving me a chance to recover from the nerve racking experience, then she let me go. Odd, people are just odd. I get that this one isn't a monster, but why does she insist that after all this time I need to have all of these experiences. The other people here don't do this to me, why Taylor? I asked Grandma.

*"Dear one, the baths feel good. They get all the dirt and sweat and grime off you and out from under your hair. It feels amazing, especially on hot days. The fly spray keeps all of the little biting bugs off you, and while it doesn't smell especially nice, it helps alot with those pesky little critters. It doesn't hurt. It just sounds funny coming out of the sprayer." She smiled at me and continued, "She works with you on picking up your feet, because they need to be trimmed and she is trying to minimize the traumatic experience for **you.** If they have to they will bring in the vet, who will sedate you heavily with the sleep drunk shot. Then the farrier will do your feet and you have to wait for a while before you can eat afterwards. If she can help you to pick up your feet and do that safely, then it's more comfortable for you. She does these things because she cares for you. She is also what they call a 'trainer'. Most people won't deal with horses that can be dangerous.*

I love you Honey, but you are dangerous for the humans to work with. It's no fault of your own, some things you don't understand, while others are things you have bad experiences with. Taylor understands that, but she is the only one who is allowed to work with you here. She is the only one who really genuinely cares, just for you. She is your person, I think."

My person? I have a person? I hadn't even considered that. I have never had a person before. But if she is the only one allowed to work with me, then she isn't really my person, right? She is stuck with me. But maybe she chose me? Why would she do that? There are other horses here that she could have chosen as her favorite. I...I have a person?

September 5

I am beyond bored of sitting here in this stall. My body feels better, even my shoulder and side are beginning to feel better. They say I have another month in this box before I can go out to pasture again. Honey could go, but she stays with me.

We watched as Joe unloaded three new horses into the quarantine today. A tall, grey, very skinny young kid that couldn't have been more than four years old. There was a short little bay roan mare with a neck brand-I know now that she's a mustang. And there was a big chestnut mare with flaxen mane and tail who was dirtier than the other two horses combined. She had the number brand on her hip, PMU.

As I watched them being led into quarantine, I realized how much I have learned in the past few months. It seems quite overwhelming to me, the amount of knowledge that I have gleaned in facing death and being pulled from it. I had no idea how many types of horses there were, none the less the destructive nature of a good portion of humans. It's pretty amazing, and pretty sad.

When Joe came back out of quarantine, I realized that Sherry was not with him. She was always with him at the kill pen. Sherry showed up a little while later, looked over towards me and Honey, smiled. She popped her head into quarantine and then went to find Joe, they spoke for a little while and then Sherry came our direction. Both Honey and I were a little wary, but I have come to trust this human. Honey went to the farthest corner of her stall- I think she had nightmares last night, she's always worse after the nightmares.

As Sherry reached my stall, she offered me a piece of apple, and said "I have a surprise for you today. Well, a friend really." I was a little nervous about this. I was wondering if they were adopting me out again, to someone I didn't know. Then I got angry as Sherry walked away back towards the ranch house. How could they just give up on Denise? Did she die? Why were they giving me away to someone else, that's always what they mean when they say a new friend. What about Honey? I looked over, but Sherry had disappeared into the house. I was reeling. I didn't want another home. I wanted...

Denise! It was her!! Sherry was pushing her out of the house in some weird rolling contraption. Her leg was all bandaged up, and she looked like they had just taken *her* out of a kill pen, but it was her! I began to dance in my stall, which turns out, hurt like hell. I guess my shoulder and ribs are not quite as healed as I thought they were. I just couldn't contain myself. Sherry rolled her over to the edge of my stall. "Easy, my girl. Don't get yourself all worked up or they won't let me visit with you. You need to heal too." Oh my heart sang.

I settled down as best I could, reached my head through the rail of my stall and Denise placed a hand on my nose. I settled into her hand, just relishing her smell. She smiled, "Well I am glad that you haven't forgotten me. I can't stay very long, but I wanted to come check on you. I miss you, love." She couldn't stand up, but I got as close to her as I could. She stroked my neck and my face for a long time. And then she began to sing. The words were choppy, as she had to catch her breath more often, but it was still beautiful and sweet. "You are the beauty of my soul. My heart attached to the end of the rope. Hoofbeats for heart beats, you are part of me. My soul, my mare, the loveliest dream. Lovely. Lady. The horses I save that save me. You are the beauty of my soul. My heart attached to the end of the rope..."

She remembered my song. After a while she looked at me and said, "My lovely Lady, I have to go now and get some rest, it's been a big day for me. But I will be back to see you and we will heal together." She kissed my nose and then Sherry pushed Denise back to an awaiting van. After they had driven off, I looked over at Honey.

Honey was emotional and I could see that she was holding back tears. "What was that song? Was that your song?" I told Honey that Denise creates a personal song for each of her horses. Blue had a song, that she would sing to him, and that was my song she had just heard. She looked off into the distance for a long time, thinking. My large friend was a phenomenally thoughtful horse. I was in high spirits for the rest of the day. Denise was still my person.

236's Journal

There were three new horses that came in today, one of them was another PMU mare. I couldn't read the numbers on her side, they headed into the barn too quickly for me to see. Grandma's person came to visit her today. She was in a weird metal rolling stall, one of her legs was all wrapped up and sticking straight out. She sang to Grandma. It was difficult for her to sing, but the song was beautiful. It was amazing to see my friend with this person. It was like they were two halves of a whole, I had never seen that before. Even though they could barely touch through the rails, it was like watching one thing, one animal that had been separated in two, but had joined again for a few moments locked in time. I can't really explain it.

I asked Grandma about the song that her person had sang to her and it was something that her person had written special, just for Grandma. I looked off, to see if I could spot Taylor. She was out working with the nurse mare foals. When I spotted her, she turned, as though she could feel me looking. From this distance I could barely see her, but I saw her smile at me. I wonder if she has a song?

Sherry's Journal

I went to pick up Denise from the hospital and take her home. We have a van that is easy access with a wheelchair. She stared out the window the entire drive. I watched her out of the corner of my eye and decided to make a detour on our way to her house. She didn't even seem to notice, off in her own little world. After a little while, we made the crunching turn onto the driveway of the rescue ranch and Denise looked over at me. I shrugged, "I thought you might want to say 'hi' to Lady before I take you home." She lit up.

She started crying and straightening up like she was going on a date, fixing her hair, brushing off her shirt. It was beautiful to see the love she had for this horse, and the emotional little girl excitement in anticipation of the moment.

We stayed as long as she was able, but as she began to tire it was time for me to take her home. She was sad to go, but seeing Lady had renewed some life to Denise and I think that it will help her heal.

September 6

It rained this morning. I love the rain, it was not very cold, but it makes everything smell new again, refreshed. I watched as the first drops fell, the old timers out in the pastures sought out shelters and the babies tore up, running around like it was their own personal party. The whole ranch smells like grass and dirt and for a while I was taken back, into my past. Back to a life I no longer know.

It had rained for three days, Duke and I were out working, tasked with bringing in the cattle herd off of the north hills. The ground was wet and slick, but Duke and I were both as sure footed as goats, I suppose I was about ten at the time. We loped along to make up ground and find the herd. There were two heelers that went with us to round up cows. Though they were generally cordial, they were fierce animals when it came to moving livestock. We found the herd in the far corner of the ranch, they were just waking up and beginning to graze, babies playing and running and bumping heads, the very young ones pushing their dams to nurse. The bull for this herd was known to be protective and we had to proceed carefully. Duke and I were adept at this herd, we had teamed the bull before. They were corrientes and Duke and gotten caught by a horn, last spring during brandings. He was a little on edge, but we were there as a team and always had each others back.

I heard Pop (Duke's rider) say, "got em" and head off to the west, around the back of them. He whistled for the heelers who followed diligently. Today my job was "Pete" the bull, keeping him from heading the herd in another direction and to keep him from goring a horse, rider or dog. We shot down the embankment towards the west flank of the herd, to keep them together and distract Pete.

Duke had reached the tail end of the herd and began pushing them from behind. Pete came straight for us, he was agile and I knew from past experiences that if you tried to get around this bull he would turn on a dime and catch you in the hip. I could feel my owner wrench on my bit to veer left, but I fought it and headed down the hill straight for that damned bull. I felt the spurs cut into my sides, but I ran and timed my actions. Just as that bull's head went down to hit me, I jumped. I tucked my feet up and as we flew over the bull, I felt one of his horns graze the underside of my left hoof. We landed, still at a full gallop and pushed that herd in the direction that we needed it to go. I heard my owner hooting and laughing. "Damn mare! Not bad!" He gave me a solid smack to the neck, which was his form of praise and I was on top of the world for a day. It was the only time I ever remember hearing the old man laugh. Pete, feeling defeated lined back up in with his herd and we didn't have any trouble from him the entire time we headed back to the main pastures.

There were always memories when it rained. It smelled like back country, no matter where you lived.

I use to hear a sound on the rooftops of the factory. It was loud and reverberated through the whole barn. I have never seen what caused it, but I remember wondering. It always sounded like it would hurt when it hit you, but I never really knew.

Today it started to rain, I heard it hitting the roof of the quarantine barn, softly at first and couldn't place the memory. I had no idea what was going on and I freaked out a little bit in my stall. Grandma asked me what was wrong and I half shouted at her, "What the hell is it?" She laughed at me, then caught herself. With a look of great concern, she uttered, "Oh my sweet Honey, have you never seen rain? Honey, it won't hurt you, it's just wet."

I calmed and watched in awe as sheets of water poured from the sky. I had been out of the factory for nearly five months and still there was so much that I have not yet experienced. It soaked my fur and I could feel it crawl along my skin, it felt wonderful and weird. I bucked up and played a little with the new sensation. It smelled sweet and I stuck my tongue out to catch some of it, it was like water I had never tasted before. I looked over eagerly to Grandma, but she was daydreaming, lost in her own world. So I stood there and just watched as the world was once again, new and interesting. The dirt changed colors from a near yellow to a deep orangey-brown. I listened as it danced on the roofs of the barn and through the trees like a thousand thundering horses.

It was raining. It was beautiful. I looked out and saw the babies running and playing. When I looked down and noticed that my feet were wet and there was water building up in the corner of my stall, not a lot, maybe just a few inches deep. I stomped, a little freaked out, and muddy water splashed up onto my belly and legs. I became a small child for a moment and continued to stomp and play in my puddle. I stopped when I saw Taylor watching me from the quarantine barn.

I stood up straight and stiff for a moment, looking at Taylor looking at me. She laughed hard, and I smiled back at her and continued to play in my newly found adventure. The rain stopped late in the afternoon and the sun peeked through the clouds, I lay next to my puddle, in the sunshine, drying out. Life, for this moment, was enchantingly good.

Chapter 15: Growth

Growing personally and helping others grow is a process that takes time. It's by far, the hardest process of any individual person or animal. Those who have the compassion to help others grow are few, but those are the ones that cultivate grace and change in our world. It's a struggle. Imagine for a moment what happens when a tree grows. A seed is placed in the ground, disturbing the earth. That seed requires care in the form of water and nutrients. The seed then breaks, ruptures and a new process of growth follows.

This tiny little thing has already had to absorb the environment around it and literally break free of the capsule containing it. Growth is a violent and difficult process, but it is one of the most beautiful things in the world. Some grow faster than others. But this tiny seed harbors a wondrous tree that provides shade and oxygen, home for animals etc. As it grows and matures it is continuously disturbing the ground beneath it, fighting for every inch of root growth and water/nutrient retention.

Growth for individuals is much like this. It's hard, it takes time, but what we offer in the process can be a benefit for many, by just our very existence in the place where we are planted.

September 20

I am tired of being in the stall. Today there was a lot of movement at the rescue. There is a small paddock, near the stalls that some of the volunteers were cleaning out and getting ready. I watched them as they worked; scrubbing the water trough, putting a feed bin in it, checking fences and repairing what needed it. They worked very efficiently for humans. Taylor and Sherry approached our stalls. Sherry haltered me and Taylor worked slowly with Honey, it only took about five minutes before she had Honey quietly haltered. They led us to the small paddock and turned us loose. Honey went and immediately found a good spot to roll, her huge body flailing around happily on the ground. She got up and shook off the dust, smiling widely. My shoulder was still sore, but I walked carefully around the paddock and checked things out. It was nice to be able to walk around.

There is a pasture next to ours that is bigger, though it does not come in contact with ours directly, it's about 10 feet away. I watched as Sherry and Taylor went back into the quarantine barn and brought out the mustang and PMU mare, Joe followed closely behind with the tall grey horse. They were turned out as a group into the neighboring pasture. An odd herd to behold indeed, though I suppose the same could have been said about me, Honey and Buck. Honey and I watched as the tall grey and the mustang ran around and kicked up, playing and getting to stretch for the first time in a month. The big PMU mare, like Honey, simply went and found a place to roll, but didn't get back up, just stretched out on the ground and went directly to sleep.

Eventually the tall grey saw us watching them and trotted over. "Hey. Ladies. My name is Go. What kind of a facility is this?"

"A rescue," I replied. He seemed a little high strung and hyper. He never really stopped moving, even when he was standing still.

"Oh, oh, okay. Well what kind of racing do we do here?"

"Racing? Darling could you stand still for a minute?"

"Oh, yeah. Sorry. I'm just pumped. I've won a lot of money for my owners. I've never met them though. I'm usually with a trainer. I've never really gone this long without, you know, whoosh. Running. I'm kind of famous."

Honey and I looked at eachother, I genuinely had no idea what this guy was talking about. Honey stifled a laugh. "Darling, where are you from?" I enquired.

"Oh, well, first I was at the breeding farm, you know raised with my ma, then I was in the big pen with the weanlings, off to the yearling sale which is a type of auction, at the trainers, then a bunch of races, then I was at another auction, then some other place and now I'm here. Hey do you want to see my tattoo?" His words all ran together a little bit and he spoke as fast as he moved. He lifted up his top lip and stretched out towards us, still talking, "Do you see it?" Yeah, we saw it. It looked like a mess of hieroglyphics, like Buck's brand only inside this one's mouth instead of on his neck.

"Are you a type of mustang?" I asked, confused as to what was going on with the brand on his lip.

He looked completely and utterly offended. "No ma'am! Indeed I am not! I..." he began trotting back and forth along the fence line, "I am the ultimate athlete, I am a thoroughbred! I was sold for sixty thousand dollars at the yearling sale. I have won two hundred thousand dollars. I am the best of the best. These fine folks here," he motioned towards Joe who was working on the tractor, "bought me for four hundred and fifty, I assume that means thousand, because, you know, racehorse." He continued to beam and prance around. I didn't have the heart to tell him that it wasn't in thousands. I'm not sure he would believe me if I tried.

Honey and I continued to watch the herd next door. The grey, strutting around like a rooster, maybe I'll call him Rooster, it makes more sense than "Go". The little mustang very carefully investigating all of her surroundings, she seemed a little shy. The big PMU mare that slept like she didn't care if she died right where she was. Odd.

236's Journal

We finally got turned out. It felt marvelous to roll and stretch out again. They turned the quarantine horses out in a pasture near us. They grey got into a conversation with Grandma, but I watched the PMU mare that was sleeping. She seemed familiar. She looks like she is older than me by a few years, but I'm pretty sure she was at the factory that I had come from.

I overheard the young grey tell Grandma that he was a racehorse. From the sound of his story he is just another industry throwaway, a byproduct of the human monsters, like many of us here. Trash that Sherry and Joe are trying to keep from dying.

Sherry's Journal
We finally got the okay from the vet to turn Lady out into a larger area. We turned them out in a small pasture near the QT barn, just in case we had to move her again, it wouldn't be far for Lady to walk. We also turned out the new horses into the pasture next to Honey

and Lady. The big off the track thoroughbred is a goofy one, but they usually are for a few weeks until they settle down. In researching his tattoo we found that he has actually won nearly a quarter of a million dollars on the track. His bail out of the kill pen was only four hundred fifty dollars. The little mustang is barely halter broke and shy, but I like her alot, I think she will be a sweet little horse once she comes around. The PMU mare, hip number 103, I'm pretty sure is from the same place as our Honey, though she seems far less aggressive. Now on to phone calls and scheduling home checks, we had seventeen adoption applications in for four horses. It's always hard to make this part of the decision, the right fit for the horse, when there are so many really good options.

September 21

That grey is an odd character. He paced the fence all day long, just back and forth down the line, he has begun to wear a path in the grass. I enquired as to what a racehorse is, he seemed awful young to do all the things that he said he had done. I had never heard of a racehorse, and I have learned of so many new things since my time here, it sparked my curiosity. Seems like he has been passed around a lot, and he's only four- not even done growing yet and pretty freshly gelded.

Once I got him to settle down a bit I asked him to tell me what a racehorse is. He seemed rather surprised at the question. "Well, I just kind of assumed everyone knew what a racehorse is. Okay so, at the breeding farm there was about a hundred of us born. We get turned out into big grass pastures with our moms. When we are weaned we are put into stalls by ourselves and halter broke, taught to lead, you know, normal stuff. Then we are turned back out until we are a little over a year old. They mess with us when they have to trim our feet, or shoot the gross paste stuff in our mouths, other than that we are pretty much left alone. When we are a little over a year, the best of us are taken out and put in stalls. They put chains over our noses, which hurt like hell and we fight the pain, so they yank harder on the chain until we give up, if we don't give up then they put it under our top lip and fight with us that way, sometimes our gums bleed, but the humans- they always win. So then they groom us and bathe us and walk us every day, if we try to fight it or get scared then we get hurt with the chain. Then we go to the big auction where there is a lot of people and they sell us for a lot of money. After that we go to the trainer. They put saddles on us and make us run straight out against other horses. They pull on our mouths and hit us with sticks to make us run faster. They chemed me once, I was sick, but had a big race coming up. That was weird- they give you a shot and it makes all your muscles shake until you can barely stand up and are sweating harder than if you had run all day. Before races they sometimes give you a shot that gets you all jacked up and pumped to run, makes you feel a little crazy, but you don't even notice if you are in pain or anything." He stopped long enough to take a breath. "I hurt my leg on the race before last. I was up for a couple of months, and then didn't run my best on this last race, my leg still hurt. But now I am here, so I don't know, all I have ever done is run." He smiled. Genuinely hopeful and continuously jittery. He was thoroughly convinced that he had given me a good definition of a racehorse, I still had no idea what he was talking about.

I looked over at Honey because I heard her crying. She was speaking to the other PMU mare. I decided to give her some space, but was close so that if she needed me, I would be there for her.

236's Journal

The PMU mare next door was up and around today. She seems confused. I called to her and she slowly turned to look at me. I introduced myself, "Hello. My name is Honey, uh I use to be 236." I turned to show the number on my hip. Her eyes got wide and she came close to the fence. "Do you have a name yet?" I asked. She just stared at me confused, worried. It was like looking into my past, though I had Grandma, and from what I could tell this horse has not bonded with anyone in her pasture. I repeated my question, "Do you have a name yet?"

"236?" Her voice was soft, and again eerily familiar. It struck me all at once, and I was taken back to the factory in a heartbeat. Down the rows of my mind, through the standing stalls, her face. I began to cry.

"103? Are you really? Is it you?" She was five years older than me. She was my sister, and while I didn't know her well, we had the same mother. When our mother had collapsed on the floor of the factory, there were three of us that cried, she was one. "What? What happened? Oh my God, I'm so glad you are safe."

"Am I safe?" She asked., looking around still very unsure of her surroundings. "There were thirteen of us that got dropped off at that weird place, and then two of them left on one trailer, five on another trailer a few days later, and then me with the two others horses that are in here." She motioned to the other horses in her pasture. "I heard we are going to die." She looked around, still confused.

"No, sister. You won't die. These ones are not monsters, they try, they are kind and patient. They give you time to learn." I realized that I was in fact speaking well of these creatures that I had so long feared. We spoke for a long time, she was thrown away for a different reason than I was. I wouldn't "take" which means I couldn't get pregnant anymore. She was thrown away because her urine wasn't "strong enough". But she was pregnant, about 4 months pregnant. Had she not been rescued, both she and her unborn foal would have been slaughtered.
*I reassured her, "you are safe here. Your baby is safe here. There's going to be reactions that you can't help, but **we** are safe here. There is so much to learn, so much to share. It's a different world, a new life. Safe."*

Sherry's Journal

Honey and our new PMU mare spent a lot of time at the fence together, today. I always try to imagine the conversations they might be having, the horses. There is so much body language and tiny little things and I often wonder if there is more to their interactions than we really understand. The grey gelding was prancing at the fence and showing off for Lady. The little mustang would run around with him from time to time, but mostly kept to herself.

September 22

When Honey told me, I was blown away. Sisters. I think this is very good for Honey, she spent a good portion of the day talking to Sister. They shared their anxiety, their worries, the things they have been surprised at. Honey shared her struggles to trust and talked about Taylor. Every time Taylor would come by to check on us, Honey would get excited and say, "That's the girl I was telling you about." It warmed my heart that there was a person that Honey felt safe with. A person that she encouraged others to feel safe with.

They spoke of the past, those who were not as lucky to be here now, their children, Sister's upcoming child. I couldn't help but think- what kind of monsters kill unborn babies on purpose? Honey explained many things that she had come to learn in our short time here, she sounded like Buck. I smiled. He would be proud of her.

Rooster and who I now know as Aspen the mustang, played and ran around for a long while and then Aspen went off by herself. I slowly made my way over towards the corner she was standing in, I introduced myself. She told me that she had been taken away from her tribe and was sent straight to the kill pens with a handful of others. Once she got here, they started working with her to get her halter broke in quarantine. She was small, maybe 13.2 but she was thick and reminded me a lot of Buck.

I told her that my old friend was a mighty mustang stallion, that he was a hero around here, helping babies, helping some of us nervous old folk. He too had been stripped of his freedom and his family, but he was a horse that healed other horses. So I shared some of Buck's wild stories with her, she seemed comforted by them and listened with interest as I passed on the legend of Buck.

September 24

Denise came to visit me again. She looked like she was feeling better, she looked healthier and had the light back in her eyes. She stroked my neck and shoulder and spoke to me for a long time. I have missed her. She is still in her rolling stall, but she seems more comfortable than the last time I saw her. I was glad that she was healing. She said it would be another few weeks yet, but that she should be able to get up and around pretty soon. She told me about her physical therapy, and while I have no idea what she was talking about with half of what she said, I was just glad that she was talking, and there with me.

I overheard Honey from time to time, explaining to Sister that Denise was my person and that we had a special bond and while not all people are good, and not all of them are monsters, some of them are special and they pick us and really love us. My friend had healed a lot in her months here. I love Honey, she is a good horse.

When Sherry came to get Denise and help her back to the van, she stopped and watched Honey and Sister who were talking to each other across the fence line. "Wow. You girls look like you could be sisters." Sherry nudged Denise softly, " I was going to name that mare, Hope, but I think I'll call her Sis." Denise smiled and pat my nose softly, "I think Sis is a good name for her. She has kind eyes." As Sherry guided Denise back to the van, I called to her. Denise looked back over her shoulder, "Love you too, my sweet Lady. I will see you again soon."
I looked back at Honey and Sister, they were staring at me. I smiled at her, "Welcome to your new life, Sis." Honey beamed while Sister smiled to herself, a little embarrassed to have the honor of a name.

Sherry's Journal
Denise called me last night and asked if I was busy, she wanted to come see Lady. While I am always busy, I will also try to always have

time for my friend.I went and got her after my morning calls and we spent some time with the girls. As we stood there, I realized just how much Honey and 103 looked like each other, the same build, face. I wonder if maybe they really are siblings. I know it happens here sometimes, the mustangs and the PMU horses that come in, families end up in the kill pens at different times. We decided to call her Sis. I wonder what the horses call each other, if we are even close.

September 25

Taylor came by to say hello to Honey, who half hid behind me. Taylor just smiled at her and headed over to the next pasture. She pulled out the grey for about an hour, and they worked across the ranch. When they came back Rooster was sweaty and seemed content. She began to approach Sister carefully and seemed surprised when Sister came right up to her. She was shy and timid, but not overly fearful. She looked sideways at Honey and Honey nodded.

Sister seemed content with that response and followed Taylor to the round pen. She too came back content, though not sweaty. Taylor headed for Aspen, my little mustang friend. Aspen was shy and tried half heartedly to avoid the contact. She wasn't tense, just concerned.

Taylor picked up on the nervousness and worked with her in the pasture. They led around for a while, Taylor touched her slowly and gently, everywhere, but when she tried to pick up Aspen's feet, Aspen kicked out like a shot and grazed Taylor's shoulder, missing her head by a breath. Taylor recovered herself without malice and gently ran her hand down Aspen's leg just until the little mare began to tense. Before she could kick out, Taylor removed her hand and gave her praise, petting her neck. "Not bad, little one."

She left the pasture and headed for our paddock. "How is my big spooky love today?" she was addressing Honey. Taylor pat my shoulder on her way by me and then stopped about three feet from my hind end, looking at Honey. Honey took two steps forward, and Taylor matched her steps, only sideways instead of towards her. Honey settled and signaled. The two of them stood for a while, with Taylor just petting Honey's neck, waiting for Honey to give the signal that she was ready to proceed. Taylor began brushing Honey with a curry she kept in her back pocket. She was talking to Honey the whole time, but it was too soft, too low for me to pick up the words. From time to time she would stop and hand Honey a treat from her pockets. Honey began searching the other pocket in hopes of knocking another treat out of them. Taylor would laugh and they continued on in their own little world for a long time. It was nice to watch Honey go from nervous to inquisitive and searching for praise, treats and contact. Taylor still had to be patient with my friend, but she trusted Taylor more than the others.

After Taylor was done with Honey she left and began hanging little signs on the pastures. It seemed like volunteers came out of nowhere and the ranch was suddenly a flurry of activity.

236's Journal

Taylor worked with all of the horses in the pasture next door. When she had brought Sister back, I asked what happened. Sister seemed a little reluctant to tell me what had happened in the round pen, and I worried for a moment that Taylor may have done something mean. I had encouraged Sister to trust, I was hoping that I had not betrayed her. I pushed and Sister told me the whole thing. "Well, she took me in a big round pen and brushed me, which felt really good. She touched me all over, and checked my teeth and mouth, no problem. You said I could trust her, so I was letting her do all these weird things. She picked up my front feet and was checking them, and cleaning the rocks out of them, when she went to pick up my back feet I shied a little bit, I eventually let her do it, but I was a little nervous. I'm sorry, that it's hard to trust with some things. I know you said it was okay, but I'm just nervous." She dropped her head a little bit, defeated and ashamed.

I looked at her in awe, she trusted Taylor simply because I said it was okay. I started laughing. "Oh Sister, don't be sad, she still can't even pick up my front feet. I try and I try, but I totally freak out. I don't mean to, I just do. I'm so proud of you!" Sister beamed, she's gonna be okay.

Taylor made her way over to me, she spent her time brushing me and telling me about her day, the other horses that she works with, how much she loves working with me. She just talked. When we were almost done, she told me that they had another Adopt An Angel Event coming up in a couple of days. She was hoping that Sister and Rooster (she calls him Billy) would find good homes. She moved towards me a little weird and laid her head on my shoulder with her arms around my neck. I looked at Grandma and nearly panicked, but Grandma nodded a little bit, so I leaned in and just stood there, a little confused. After Taylor left I asked Grandma what that was all about. Taylor had hugged me. Maybe she is my person.

Sherry's Journal

I watch Taylor and Honey together often. Taylor works the other horses beautifully, but she and Honey have a special bond. There is something more there than just training progress and I don't think that either of them want to admit it, even though I am sure that it is evident to more than just me. Lady watches them together and seems pleased. It's hard to explain, it's like she is happy for her friend. Maybe I am projecting those emotions, but that is how it always seems. I hope they see it one day, that they, Taylor and Honey are bonded whether they like it or not.

Chapter 16: Seasons

There are seasons for everything. Each individual adjusts to these changing seasons in their own way. With each, they carry their own beauty and struggles. As cooler weather sets in and the days grow shorter there are many things that need to be considered by horse people and rescues that are not a consideration for most other people. Some of these things are stockpiling hay in case you are not able to get out and get hay, whether to blanket horses, increasing feed for older horses to try and assist with their ability to keep weight on, how very young horses will adapt to the changed environment, or if they will struggle to meet the warmth production of their bodies, if you have enough hay at any given time to get through a period of time when roads may be flooded or blocked by snow, making sure that there is enough medical supplies in case a vet can't get out to you due to inclimate weather. These are all necessary considerations for horse people, and more so for rescues and sanctuaries where they care for compromised horses, unhandled horses, etc.

People forget that with the care of these animals comes not only a cost for care, but scrutiny from the public for non-care. Rescuers bear this burden gladly, but be reminded that they do not get days off, just because the weather is bad for the rest of society on any given day. They are always out, caring for their charge.

September 27

The last few days have been a craze of activity. Everyone is getting ready for the Adopt An Angel event which takes place in the spring and in the fall. They placed signs on all of the stalls and pastures that have horses in them, I wonder what they will do with the babies now that Buck is not here. I looked to the rose garden, I missed him. It was the day before the event in spring, that I met Buck and our little herd began to take shape.

Horses were being taken out, washed, groomed, ridden around the property. People were working on fences and double checking signs. There were signs on our paddock too. There was a red sign with Honey's name on it and a blue sign with mine. Most of the horses had green, yellow, or orange signs, though I did see a red sign from time to time. What I did not see were any other blue signs, only mine. I wonder what the colors mean.

236's Journal

Rooster is a very high strung but seemingly good tempered young horse, I hope that someone sees the good in him and gives him a nice home. He has the chance to be adopted tomorrow. Sister is nervous about meeting people, but I reassured her. Knowing that Grandma's person is amazing, I know that if Sister gets adopted she and her foal will have a wonderful home. I don't think I will ever be adopted, Like Buck I think that this place will forever be my home, and I am okay with that. It has taken me many months to trust Taylor really at all, and I am not sure that I would be able to trust another human. They still scare me, but Taylor is okay. I have heard the volunteers speak, they say that I am dangerous and that Taylor is the only one allowed to handle me. It's odd to me, I have heard them say that I scare them, but most of what I do is because I am scared of **them**. I would not have thought that humans were afraid of anything, it makes me sad a little bit that they can't see that I am just afraid. I am glad that Taylor sees it though. A few of the nurse mare foals went by. They said hello as they passed. They were growing so fast! One of them said that he was sorry about what happened to Buck. I just told them to be good and to find themselves good humans to take care of them.

They laughed and giggled and went on their way to the line of stalls for people to meet them. It warmed my heart. I looked out across the pastures and saw Tundra and one other little filly left in the pasture. They were watching their friends leave. Tundra was still small. I called to her to say hello. She lifted her head way up high and hollered back. When Tundra hollered back, Aspen brought her head up fast, her eyes wide. She walked over to the fence and stared into the distance. She called, her voice caught, and she waited. Tundra called back. Aspen began to cry, hard.

I asked Aspen if she was okay, if she knew the feisty little Tundra. Aspen smiled, though she was still crying. "She was my sister's daughter. We were from the same tribe. Her mother was injured during the round up. The giant bird kept pushing us, we couldn't go back. Tundra was pushed on with the herd, she stayed with me in the pens. I don't know what happened to her mom. She had fallen pretty hard and couldn't get back up. She was still down when I looked over as we were running. But I had worried about little Tundra when she was taken with a large group of horses. I ended up going with a large group of horses later on, after no one adopted me from the pens." Aspen *sighed, but was still looking out across the ranch to little Tundra. "They kill us you know. All of the mares that were purchased and shipped to slaughter were pregnant. They and their unborn babies were killed for convenience. They don't care at all what happens to us, we are just in their way, a waste. They replace us with cows. They blame us for the things that the cows do, like overgrazing, destruction of land, all sorts of things. We have lived peacefully in that valley for many many generations, in much larger herds than there are now. But they say that* **we** *are the problem. That little girl over there, is what is left of my family. And she will never see her mom or her herd again. It just breaks my heart. But I am glad that she made it here, that she will live, even if not free."*

My heart broke for this family, I think the PMU horses have a very similar loss to the mustangs. Our lives are very different, but our loss is much the same.

Sherry's Journal

It's that time again, it came fast. It's a little harder knowing that Buck will not be here this year, but I am excited for the futures of the horses that may find homes tomorrow.

September 28

So, today was the day. The rescue's Adopt An Angel event. There were a lot of people. Taylor had come by really early, before the sun was even up and spent some time with Honey, talked to her. Once people had started coming, there was a young lady that had come over and was reading all of the signs. She stopped at Rooster, Aspen and Sister's pasture. Rooster rushed the fence, so excited that it was evident to all that he could barely wait to meet everyone who came by. The young lady laughed and gave him a scratch on his nose. Sherry came by and they were talking about him. I heard the girl ask if Rooster was broke, Sherry told her that he was broke for the track, but hadn't been trained beyond that yet. They spoke some more and then Sherry left. The young lady came in between the space in our pastures and Rooster followed at a trot. She smiled at him and said, "ready, boy?" and he backed his butt up into the corner. They took off like a shot, the girl and Rooster running back and forth along the length of the fence. Honey and I watched the two of them playing through the fence and laughed.

I think Rooster found someone who is as energetic as he is. When she walked away Rooster called after her. "Hey! Hey girl! Come back! Play with me!" He was dancing in place. She looked over her shoulder and smiled, but continued walking. After about 2 hours that young girl came back with a blue sign. She hung it on his fence and kissed him on the nose, "We have to do a homecheck and they have to check my references, it'll be a few days, but you are mine now." Rooster was so excited, dancing around working himself all up again. He had a person.

Blue meant you had a person. BLUE MEANT YOU HAD A PERSON! MY SIGN WAS BLUE!
Denise was still my person!

Taylor eventually came by with a woman. She was strongly built, she had jeans and long dark hair. There was a kindness, a gentleness about her. Taylor led her over to Sister's pasture. Rooster as always rushed the pasture to say hello, he was bobbing his head, and dancing across the fence- struttin like the rooster he was. I heard Taylor and the woman talking.

"You had mentioned that you were looking for a special needs horse. This big girl here, is Sis. She is a PMU mare. She is in foal, about 4 months along. And while she is not necessarily 'special needs' she will need patience and a very special person to give her the time she requires, to learn how to be a horse. I don't know that she will ever be a riding horse, she's nearly 20, but she will have a beautiful foal that would probably make a nice riding prospect. This mare is a love, she wants to trust, but needs time and patience."

The woman with Taylor, looked at Sister and put out her hand. Sister stood a little ways off but stretched out her neck and sniffed at the womans hand. The woman smiled at her. "May I go in?" She looked at Taylor.
"Of course. Just watch out for Billy, the grey gelding, he can be a little pushy. He's nice, just pushy." Taylor stood by as the woman went in and spoke with Sister. She didn't halter her, but faced Sister and took a step sideways, Sister mirrored the move, anticipating the motion. She pet Sister for a little while, with Rooster constantly putting himself into the middle of the interaction. Taylor went in and haltered Rooster, leading him away a little bit to give Sister and this new person some space. She smiled at Sister, "What you do think big girl? Are you willing to give me a chance? You and your baby would have a forever home with me." The woman reached down and placed her hand on Sister's belly, gently rubbed her belly and whispered something to Sister. Sister just leaned in appreciating the rubbing on the scratch that she can't reach. She groaned a little bit in bliss and everyone laughed. After a while, her sign too was replaced

with a blue sign. By the evening more blue signs showed up. As things began to wind down, the volunteers came and threw feed. Aspen still had an orange sign. She seemed okay with not being chosen this time around.

Honey was semi traumatized by all of the people which had come through. Most of the day she hid in the back of our paddock, and was now happily laying in the hay pile, eating. Sister was a little nervous but excited, "This will be my first baby that I get to raise, that will be born in a safe place!"

"Last baby." Honey piped in between mouthfuls of food.

"What?" Sister looked confused.

Honey heaved her bulk up off the ground and stretched. She walked over to the fence, looked at her sister lovingly, "You don't have to have any more babies, Sister. You will have your baby in a safe place, then you will be free to just be a horse. You don't have to keep having babies. We are free from being a factory."

Sister looked surprised and even more excited, she hadn't thought of that part. She began to cry, tears of pure joy.

236's Journal

Sister and Rooster were both adopted today. They will only be here for a few more days. It seems like this time has been so short, and I wonder what they are going to do with Aspen after Sister and Rooster go to their new homes. I feel bad for that little mare. I looked over towards Tundra's pasture that currently held just her and one other little filly.

One of the signs on the pasture was blue, but they were too far away to see which one. Maybe they could put Aspen in with me and Grandma,

although Grandma has a blue sign too. I like the mustangs, maybe I
will get along with this little one like Buck and I had. God I miss that
crazy old fool.

September 29

Rooster got a bath this afternoon and the farrier came out to clean
up his feet. I got a trim for the first time since breaking my shoulder.
While I was a little stiff, I was able to get my leg up where he needed
me to be. It was nice to have my feet done. Sis was next, Taylor
worked with her slowly and the farrier was patient, they got her front
ones done pretty well, but she had to be lightly sedated for her back
feet, she just wasn't to that point yet. They took a break and sat on
the back of the farrier's truck and ate some lunch. The farrier asked
about doing Aspen, but Taylor assured him that Aspen was not
ready yet. They moved on to do the other horses on their list for the
week.

Next line of duty were baths, or attempts at bathing. One of the
volunteers came and got Rooster. After about half an hour Rooster
came back clean and shiny with his tail brushed out and his attitude
and ego firmly intact. Sherry and one of the volunteers came and got
Sister. It took about 2 hours, we heard a little commotion and Sherry
brought Sister back wet and one leg was a still just a little soapy. She
looked deflated. Sherry was nearly as wet as Sister. I choked on my
laughter, Honey choked up a little bit as well and said, "Well, again
you made it further than I have." At which point all three of us broke
out in roarous laughter.

Rooster came over when he heard us laughing, looked at Sister with disgust, "What the hell happened to you?"

Sister was quick on the uptake and disarmed Rooster's ego, "Well they tried to kill me with acid, but I got them first." Honey and I had to turn away to keep from laughing, Rooster just looked at Sister absolutely horrified and walked away to keep his coat pristine. Sister found the best dirt spot in the pasture and proceeded to cake mud onto herself by rolling repeatedly. We spent a lot of time throughout the day discussing what Sister and Roster thought their new homes would be like. Both of them were very excited, and both were very nervous.

Aspen was hunkered down in a corner. Honey went over near the fence and talked to her for a long time. The rest of us talked about our people. Our herds suddenly had a very definitive split that could almost be felt.

236's Journal

Rooster got a bath, now he is shiny and smells funny. They tried to give Sister a bath, but that did not go as smoothly, given that she was still wet and kinda soapy when she came back, and so was Sherry. Now Sister just looks like a walking wall of mud. A weird thing happened today, a rift. For a while we became two separate herds, Grandma, Sister and Rooster were a herd; Aspen and I were a herd. The adopted and the outcast. It was an unanticipated transition.

I noticed that Aspen was standing in a corner by herself, so I went to talk to her. I was so tired of listening to the other three talk about their people, what they think it will be like in a new home. I am not one of them when it comes to that, so I would rather be with Aspen, especially since she seems so down today. "Hey, you okay?" *I checked.*

"Nobody wanted me. Sister and Rooster are going to new homes soon, but nobody wanted me. I am really conflicted about that though, because while I can't stand them I thought **someone** might want me." *She began to sniffle.*

'Well, hell girl. You have a lot more potential than I do, that's for sure. You at least are adoptable, and basically just need to wait it out. I will never get to that point- I'm 'unadoptable'. The people are afraid of me, well everyone except Taylor. Cheer up! I am going to need someone to keep me company when they all go. Grandma will be leaving eventually too, back to her person." Aspen and I spoke for most of the afternoon. Two separate herds, with two separate destinies.

Sherry's Journal

I love to watch the horses after the adoption event. It's like so many of them know that they are on their way to new lives. There is an anticipation throughout the ranch that can be felt. I always look forward to the updates from adopters, knowing that a life saved is a life changed.

September 30

Taylor came by and told us to say our goodbyes, Sister and Rooster's people would be here in the evening to pick them up. There was a lot of emotion, especially between Honey and Sister. In the afternoon Taylor and Sherry came and took Rooster and Sister over to the stalls to wait for their respective people. As Sister passed by our paddock, she and Honey touched noses for a moment, an intimate heartbeat, and then they were off.

The little one in with Tundra was also brought up and put in a stall. Taylor headed back down to Tundra and led her up towards us. We assumed she was going in with the other babies, and perhaps that was the original intention. Aspen ran to the fence to say hello to her little niece. Tundra, strong for her tiny stature, pulled Taylor nearly off her feet, over to the corner of Aspen's pasture. Taylor allowed them to say their hellos for a few minutes and watched as Aspen and Tundra touched noses and Tundra ran her side along the corner of Aspen's fence. Both Honey and I were trying to mask our emotions, but we were both watching, overwhelmed by the moment. It was an emotional reunion to watch. This tiny little mustang filly, torn from her family; the entirety of her herd devastated by the human need to destroy and consume everything around them. Aspen was the only other one from the herd to have survived, their line was broken, no longer existing in the wild. Aspen was trying to reassure Tundra through held back tears. Taylor watched the interaction with great interest. After about five minutes she got on the phone. She was talking to someone while Aspen and Tundra were trying to groom each other from opposite sides of the fence. Taylor's part of the conversation was all that we heard.

"Can you see me from where you are?"…"Do you see the horses?"…"Yeah that's what it's looking like to me too, it does happen."…Okay cool. I'll do that." And then the conversation ended. Taylor looked at Tundra, "Well little one, looks like there has been a slight change of plans." Tundra, very solemnly walked back over to Taylor and was preparing herself to leave.

Taylor put Tundra in with Aspen. The two mustangs immediately began nosing each other all over. "I can't believe how big you have gotten!" She announced to Tundra. Honey and I both looked a little surprised, Tundra was still very tiny, though now that I think of it, Aspen is pretty small to begin with also, and she is full grown. Taylor watched for a minute, nodded and left to prepare other horses that had been adopted the previous day.

It was the most alive I had ever seen Aspen, she was running and playing and grooming with little Tundra, from time to time Sherry would come over and take pictures. At one point Sherry stopped and just stood at the fence to watch them for a long time. Joe came and joined her.

"I wish they would just leave these beautiful creatures alone." Joe's words were full of emotion. "I called the holding facility, and talked to them about the brands on the girls here. Apparently that kill buyer bought the whole herd. These are the only two left from that herd, there are no more in the wild. There are no more anywhere. If something is not done, we will lose all of our mustangs to the meat trade. I just can't believe they would decimate an entire family like that. For what?" His little rant was laced with sadness and anger. He sighed "At least these two have each other. I will change the paperwork on them to make sure they get adopted out together when the time comes. The same thing is happening in Nevada, where Buck was, those people are destroying an entire ecosystem." Joe and Sherry stood there and watched the mustangs for a long time before they left. Rooster's owner had arrived and was talking to him and packing him full of carrots at the gate to his stall.

Honey and I watched as one after the other horses were loaded, by themselves, some in pairs, onto trailers and taken away, to new homes, to new adventures, to new lives. The last one to arrive was Sister's new owner. She walked up to Sister's stall and was stroking her neck, scratching her belly. Sister checked pockets and was as gentle with her lady as her lady was with her. Her new owner put a halter on her and began to lead her to the trailer when Sister slammed on her brakes. Her adopter just waited patiently, encouraged her, without forcing her. Sister loaded quietly onto the trailer. And then silence and the calm that comes only after exhaustive work, settled over the ranch.

As the sun set I looked over to see little Tundra curled up and sleeping alongside Aspen, both seemed quieter and happier. There was a chill in the air and it smelled like the snow was coming soon. I laid down and curled up back to back against Honey.

Sherry's Journal.
A heartfelt reunion. I shed silent tears as we watched Taylor reunite our mustang filly with what is left of her herd, Aspen. It was achingly beautiful to see them touch, caress and love on eachother so completely. I wish we could save them all. Joe came and stood with me for a while. He had one of his rare emotional moments. He is usually stoic, but he is far more passionate than I give him credit for. Sometimes I forget he loves this work as much as I do, especially the mustangs.

October 1

It was cold this morning and the clouds were a bright blue, snow is on its way for sure. My stifle ached a little when I got up and there was a light frost on the grass. It was quiet at the ranch, except for the sound of horses in the morning and the feed truck that came through. It had been a rough night. In my dreams I relived the scene on the side of the road, but rather than the vet putting Blue down, as had been done in reality; it was Duke, lying there and I woke up when the old man shot him. I remember thinking at the time, as violent as it looked, it was probably the nicest thing that old man had ever done for a horse. Duke had been in a lot of pain and would have died horribly and painfully if they had waited for a vet. Perhaps that was the turning point in my future. I don't know, but the dream caused me to wake in a rather emotionally charged mood. I was a little short with everyone all day. In the evening I apologized to Honey for my being so cranky and explained to her all that had happened in my dreams last night. She too had dreams, and often nightmares. She just snuggled up against me, she understood.

236's Journal

Grandma and I both had a rough night last night. The family reunions of the last few weeks have had their effect on all of us. Grandma dreamed of the accident on the road. Today was the first time she really opened up about some of what had happened there. It was heartbreaking to listen to her recount the details and the realization that in a moment her heaven was turned into hell by some stupid monster who thought they were funny. I too dreamed last night, though I didn't go into details with Grandma. It didn't seem that she needed more emotions put on her today.

I was 18 months old when they bred me the first time. I didn't know what was going on. It was a nightmare unto itself. I was just a baby. They pushed me into one of the standing stalls between these two other mare who were huge compared to me. They put the catheter in and from then on I spent my life in that stall. Stall number 236. I grew up there, lived there, ate there. Never moving around, not sleeping. I am surprised that I survived, and it is ironic to me that it was when they sent me away to kill me, that I finally got a name, a hope. Rather than meet the horrific end they had intended for me as a byproduct of and industry, I came here, to live, having to learn how not only to be a horse, but to see humans in a different light. Not getting pregnant saved my life from a violent life and a violent death. So many days and nights in that factory that I wished for death, a few weeks that I had prepared myself to meet death.

*Now here, only a few short months later **wanting** to live, encouraging Sister to trust the humans. I would have never thought that I would be the horse I am today. It's quite amazing really. The people who work here, they don't just save horses. They saved **me.** The violent, fearful horse that didn't even know how to be a horse, these people gave **me** a chance to live.*

Chapter 17: Unexpected

We don't always see the reason for things. Sometimes things happen that are unexpected. These are the things that make life, life. The unanticipated breaks from routine, the small surprises- both good and bad. Routine and patter and the things that form the borders of our lives. We tend to anticipate whether things will trend or not, we try to place life into a patterned box of our expectations.

Rarely does life comply with what we think it should do. Often times we are surprised by the ebb and flow of our personal tides. The unexpected events in our lives make room for us to grow, change, adapt. Sometimes they fracture our securities and sometimes they allow us to change the way that we view the world around us, but never does the unexpected fail. It is an ever present aspect of everything that exists.

October 3

The first snow of the season left a soft white blanket on everything within view. It was not an intense or harsh storm, just a dusting of the earth and all that was around. My shoulder and my stifle both made themselves known in the cold. The sky lay dark and ominous, a promise for more to come.

Honey was slightly panicked through the night, as she has never been in snow before. Much like the rain, my friend still has much to learn about being alive in something other than a 4x8 box. As I reassured her she began to run around in the snow, sticking her tongue out and generally exploring this newfound freedom to be. It was beautiful to watch and I renewed my appreciation for being a horse that had lived and worked outside for the majority of my life. Honey's large lumbering body was thundering around our pasture. She was suddenly a young filly in a huge mature body, bucking up kicking out and disturbing the pattern of the light little flakes of white. It was a dance in the darkness that only I and a few others were lucky enough to witness.

Taylor came to our pasture, all bundled up against the cold. Honey was a little taken aback by the sheer bulk of the tiny woman and was unsure as to how to react. Taylor reassured her with her words and approached calmly and carefully as usual. There was no halter in her hands, but there was something in her back pocket, rolled up under her jacket. It's shape was similar to a carrot, but thicker. I could see the shape of it and Taylor was awaiting Honey's approach with an unusual anticipation.

As Honey came up to Taylor, she investigated her poofy form, pushing against the jacket, startling when it made a weird noise or the sensation was off. Taylor just allowed her to check it all out and occasionally laughed. When Honey was content in her safety she stood next to Taylor. Taylor laid her head against Honey's shoulder and just stood there in the snow for a long time. Eventually she looked over at Honey, "I have a surprise for you." She backed up a step so as not to scare my friend. Slowly she lifted the back of her jacket and pulled out the rolled up paper that had been there. She showed it to Honey, more for the moment than because she thought we could read. The paper was blue. My eyes widened.

236's Journal

Taylor came to spend time with me today, as we do often. It smelled like her but she appeared significantly larger than she had previously. There was a lot of bulk to her. I investigated her jacket and her hat, sometimes the jacket would make a scratchy noise that would scare me and I would take off, gather myself and go back to see what this thing was all about. Grandma was behind Taylor and kept looking at her pockets. I thought perhaps Taylor had treats, so I checked her other pockets, but couldn't find anything.

After a while Taylor laid her head on my shoulder. I still tense, but I am eerily comforted by this particular human. She backed up a few steps and said that she had a surprise for me. She pulled a blue piece of paper out of her back pocket and unrolled it. Grandma was staring, mouth agape.

Taylor's eyes began to tear up a little bit, "You have been adopted Honey. The okay came in this morning." I was in shock. No one had stopped at our pasture or looked at me or talked to me during the adoption event. Nobody wanted me, I was the monster, the horse that everyone was scared of. I was a sanctuary horse. Who could have possibly adopted me? I was suddenly nervous and anxious about the potential of a new person invading my life. I didn't know how to feel, or what to do in that moment. I just looked at the paper in her hand, and then looked into her eyes. My concern and confusion was evident on my face.

Taylor was crying full force now, "It'll be okay love. It will be okay. I know you still have a long way to go, and who knows maybe you will never fully trust. I wouldn't blame you for that. But they are all things that we can work on." I was confused. How were we going to work on things if I was gone? Was my adopter going to let me stay here and let me continue to work with Taylor? Why would they let someone adopt "The dangerous horse?"

Taylor could read my tension. "Easy momma. Don't stress. There is nothing to be afraid of. You belong to me now. We will always be a team, you and me." Her voice was cracking, "You will stay here with us until it's time for Lady to go home to Denise. You will be going with Lady, I am going to help Denise out by coming out to feed you guys and take care of you. She has agreed to a board trade...so that I can keep my horse there in exchange for help. You know, because she is older and she is still recovering from her injuries. But you have a home, and I am your person, and you are my horse now." Taylor didn't even concern herself with my reactivity for a moment and threw her arms around my neck. This was for real, I have a home, a person, a purpose.

*I was in shock. Taylor had adopted me. She was my person. There was so much emotion going on in me that I was overwhelmed. Someone did want me- **she** wanted me. I had a home. There in the snow and the cold, I stood with **my** person. My person, who didn't mind that I was scared. My person who didn't mind that I was nervous or still learning. I looked over at Aspen and Tundra, then to Grandma. Everyone was crying and smiling. The horse that no one wanted, sanctioned for slaughter, destined to die...was loved.*

Sherry's Journal

Taylor and I spoke for a long time over the past few days. She decided that she wanted to adopt Honey. Her and Denise worked it out to where Honey could stay at Denise's place, with Lady. Taylor would help Denise while she continued towards healing from her injuries. I watched with tears streaming down my face as Taylor approached Honey and told her that they were now a family. Had it been anybody else, I would have said "no". But the two of them are connected on a far deeper level than even I realized, I think. I think Honey understood, and I could swear I saw her cry tears of joy. She was loved, she is wanted. She is family. It was one of the most beautiful things I have ever witnessed in my years of doing this.

October 4th

Everyone has been on a high since the announcement that Honey had been adopted by Taylor. It was an amazing moment and I don't think I will ever forget it. I think Honey is still in shock. Taylor comes by regularly and gives her treats. It is a happy time.

The snow has melted but it is still cold, the saving grace is that the sun is out today and is giving us a soft warmth. To look around you would think it's a graveyard, the majority of the horses on the ranch are laid out and bathing in the sunlight.

Denise came today. She is out of her wheelchair and is carefully guiding herself forward in what she calls a walker. It's like a driving cart that they put on her backwards. It looks odd and she moves slowly, but she is getting better and I am so very glad for that. Sherry walked with her over to our paddock. I half walked half trotted over to meet her at the gate. She reached her hand out and I placed the side of my face into it. "Hello my sweet Lady. I heard that Taylor has told you guys about the exciting news."

She looked at Honey, "I hope you like it at my home. I know Lady will be glad to have you, her very special friend, as company. I will be ever grateful for Taylor's help." Denise turned her attention back to me, "I am on my way to physical therapy, but I wanted to stop by and see you, my love." she gave me a soft scratch on my neck and then made her way laboriously back to the car that had brought her. I missed my person already, but I am glad that she was able to come see me. Hopefully it would not be much longer before I could go home. It would be Honey's home too now.

I thought about Hero's tree. I would have to remember to tell Honey about Hero, just as Blue had told me. I wondered what happened to Blue, I wonder where he got buried. I don't know if he had gotten his tree, if he was in the field with the mare he called momma. My heart broke for a moment. Well even if he didn't get a tree, he would never be forgotten, not by me. I would tell his story and he would live on.

236's Journal

I am excited and nervous about this new adventure that awaits me. I really never thought it would ever come to this. I have a person and soon I will have a home. It's the fulfillment of a dream that I didn't even know I had. It was all too much to take in, really. I watched Taylor work out in the pastures with the other horses, but my view of the world was a little different today. She was mine. I would be going home with Grandma and would not be alone.

I was still afraid of people for the most part, but I no longer had to fear loneliness. It was an unfamiliar concept that I had a hard time grasping. I half thought this was maybe all a dream, that I would wake up and still be in the factory. My flashbacks are not as often as they use to be, though they still make their way to the forefront of my mind from time to time. I am very nervous, but I am glad that Grandma will be there with me. I'm glad that Taylor will continue to be patient with me. I am loved, but even more than that, I have learned to love.

October 5

I am feeling this cold more than I have in the past, perhaps it was from my accident, I don't know but my stifle, my side and my shoulder are certainly more achy than they have ever been. I am moving slower and it seems like this fall may be colder than the last one, we aren't even in to winter yet. I have noticed that I lost some weight since my accident, I am not as fleshy as I once was. I have aged more these past few months than I have in 22 years. I guess being passed from auction house, to kill pen to rescue to a home and back again has taken its toll on me. I am tired. Today I feel old. It makes me think of Buck, he was 30 and still as wry and feisty as ever. I am saddened that he is gone but I am glad that he is finally back with his herd on the sky range.

Honey noticed that I was having a rougher time today and stuck very close to me. I don't know why I am so tired. She huddled side by side to keep me warmer and even brought me some of the hay so that I wouldn't have to walk so far. She is by far one of the best horses I have ever had the pleasure of knowing.

236's Journal

Grandma is not doing very well. She has lost some weight and is straining harder to move around today. I think her accident did more damage, wore her out more quickly. I worry about her. I tried to take care of her as best I could, and I know she is in more pain than she is showing, because that is our way. It is hard to see my friend like this, she has gotten more grey in just a month or so, and I worry that she is not as strong as she wants to be.

October 6

Taylor came to the paddock early this morning. She had a halter and came in slowly. She furrowed her brow, knowing that something wasn't quite right. She made a phone call and shortly afterwards, Sherry came walking up to the pasture. She took one look at me and was on the phone. They took me to the infirmary barn, where the vet has all of his stuff set up. They put me in a stall, took blood, gave me a shot and left the needle in my neck. The vet came back after about an hour with results from the bloodwork. He talked with Sherry and Taylor, and as he was speaking a car pulled up with Denise in it. She made her way towards the barn. She had a look of intense worry on her face. She looked at me long and hard, and headed over to talk to the vet. They spoke for what seemed like hours, it was in actuality maybe ten minutes. I heard the vet say that I had an infection but I didn't catch much more, I was having trouble focusing.

Denise came over to me, she was crying. "You gotta be strong now, my love. It'll will be a while longer before you are able to come home. You have to be strong for me." I lifted my head and nudged her. She stayed with me for the rest of the day as the vets gave me fluids, antibiotics, took x rays and ultrasounds of my sides. Once they finished with me, they took me out of the stall and put a blanket on me. It was warm and had some pattern on it. They took me back to quarantine. Once I got settled in I watched as Denise and Taylor spoke just outside of the barn.

236's Journal

Grandma was really sick today, she was kind of confused and her nose was super runny. Taylor had come early, and had halters in her hands, but when she saw Grandma she gathered the troops. They took Grandma into the vet barn and were there all day.

I noticed that there was a trailer with fresh shavings and the door open, Taylor had come with halters. I think we were supposed to go home today, instead I stood at the gate to my paddock and spent my time staring at the vet barn and quarantine. Denise and Taylor were standing outside the quarantine barn, after they moved Grandma. She had some sort of poofy thing on, like Taylor had on the day she told me I belonged.

I don't feel like I belong right now, I feel alone. They usually take me with Grandma if she gets moved anywhere at the rescue. It's odd, I use to be by myself all the time, in a large group of horses, but by myself, until I met Grandma. Now it makes me anxious to be alone. I have gotten a little better, I think. But it is still unnerving.

Taylor came over in the afternoon, "Sorry, my girl. We were hoping to get you guys home today. Lady is sick and she has to stay here for a while. We figured you wouldn't want to go to a new place all by yourself, so we will get you guys home when Lady is feeling better. She has a respiratory infection and is running a little fever, but she will be okay, I think." Taylor didn't reach out to touch me, she rarely did, she just stood near the fence and let me touch her if I wanted to. She respected my anxiety about people and would allow me to make the choice of contact, which I have come to do a little more.

Sherry's Journal

As soon as you think you can breathe, something happens. Isn't that the way life always goes. These horses sometimes just can't seem to catch a break. Lady is sick, very sick and we just aren't sure if she is going to make it. She is a fighter and I have no doubt that if she has anything to say about this, she will pull through, but it's always heartbreaking to me, when a horse gets to almost. Almost there, almost happy, almost made it. I pray this is not one of those cases.

October 8

Back in quarantine. I felt a little better today, not as achy, but I am still tired. They give me grain with medicine in it, I know because I can smell the medicine. I'm not all that hungry though, I try to be upbeat and happy but there is just no desire to do so. There are two other horses in quarantine with me, an appy and what looks like a little quarter horse, except he moves funny. I don't feel like talking today though, maybe I'll ask their names tomorrow.

236's Journal

Aspen and Tundra keep asking me about Grandma. They want to know what happened, where she is, if she is coming back. I told them that she was sick, that she is coming back, but I don't know when. We spent the rest of the day with them telling me stories about their tribe, out on the range. Like Buck, they had many adventures, Tundra's mother was their stallion's favorite mare, they were always together.

There are strong family bonds with the mustangs, closer than any other breed that I have ever encountered, they remember every horse, they remember every family member and their unique attributes. It's something special that connects them as a unit far beyond bonding and closeness. The friends they make as foals stay their friends even into their older years, regardless of whether they switch herds or not. It's an interesting dynamic.

Aspen told me about the day that Tundra was born. Her mother went into labor and the herd gathered around to protect the mare and foal while it was being born. The whole tribe would help when a baby was coming. Tundra, like the rest of the horses in their herd, was born small but very sturdy. She stood fast, and before she could even nurse, everyone gathered around to welcome the new little baby into the tribe. It was a family affair, not just a mother and baby in a pen. The whole tribe would help raise the foal, other mares would often nurse foals that weren't theirs. They were a uit, a tribe, a single entity that simply had different parts, less like a family and more like a body. Tundra was only 2 months old when the death bird came.

Hearing het story told from the point of view of a baby is far different than it was when Buck told it, somehow more heartbreaking, more real, more painful. Tundra's tiny voice was solemn, but powerful. "We were grazing when the alert went out that there was danger. My mother pushed me out in front of her and our herd began to run. I tried to keep up, but I was getting tired quickly. Horses were stumbling and getting back up and running. Lilly, the other baby and I were getting jostled and slammed in between the horses in the herd. They didn't mean to bang into us, they were just as scared as we were. I was screaming to my mom asking her what was going on and she kept saying 'I don't know baby. I don't know what that is. Stay close, keep up.' Mommy was out of breath, she was getting tired, we all were.

Daddy was trying his best to keep the herd together and when Momma fell she went head over heels. Daddy tried to go back , but the scary bird just kept pushing hard wind down on us and chasing us across the valley. I kept screaming for my momma, but she didn't get back up. Daddy said to stay with my aunts, that he would go find her when this was all over. He was a good daddy, he tried to keep us safe. One of the mares was bleeding down her leg, she had gotten snagged on something as we were running, I think. By the time that Daddy saw the fencing it was too late." Tundra paused, "He tried to warn us to turn around, to watch out, but we were all going too fast. One of my aunties got tangled in the fence, but the bird didn't stop- there were horses with two heads that spit ropes, one of them got my auntie that was stuck in the fence and started strangling her with it's rope thing. I screamed for her, but she just yelled back in kind of a gurgling noise, 'run baby!'

The pushed us into small pens where we were all crammed together. Daddy tried to push the fence to get us out, but he couldn't do it, he tried to jump the fence but it was too high and he fell over backwards and hurt himself pretty bad. They split us all up, put us one by one through a tiny little opening and burnt our necks with the cold fire. After a few days a man came and bought a bunch of us and took us to the kill pen. Daddy died."

I think they were trying to distract me from Grandma being sick, but my heart hurt now more than ever, for Grandma, and for these mustangs. I am so torn when it comes to people. There are people, but I still think a lot of them are monsters.

October 9

The barn was cold this morning. I could see that there was frost on the ground outside. I felt a little better yesterday, but today I feel horrible. My chest is tight and I have a headache. At least the blanket they put on me is warm. I am depressed and it seems like I am never going to make it back home. Sherry came in early this morning and brought me a warm mash. I was only going to take a little bit of it, but it was warm and good and before I knew it, I had finished it. Maybe it will help.

I spoke with the little gelding next to me, Pancho is his name. He is a Paso Fino, I have never heard of them before. He says that he moves "funny" because he is gaited. He has been in shows, parades, on trail. I guess his person died and the rest of his person's family didn't want or know what to do with a horse. He ended up at the auction, off to the kill pen when no one else bid on him, and now he's here. It's odd to me how many good horses, working honest horses end up at the kill pens.

The big appy mare off in the corner is shy, but she seems to be kind in general. She was a broodmare, she made babies for the shows. She is 12 and while she showed as a baby, mostly has only ever been a momma. She says she is a halter horse, her legs are small for her frame and she seems to carry more bulk than other horses. She was shown in halter as a baby and then turned in to a baby maker.

So many horses thrown away. After Sherry had fed us this morning, she just hung out with us for a while and drank her coffee. I could smell it from my stall, maybe it's just us ranch horses, but the smell of coffee is definitely a unique smell on humans, sometimes it's sweet, sometimes it's bitter, but there is always that underlying smell of coffee. Joe came in after a while and sat with her.

"You know, as hard as we try, we can't save them all." He whispered, as he wrapped an arm around her.

Sherry sighed, " I know. We can barely save a fraction of what is shipped to slaughter. It just breaks my heart, such beautiful creatures, such horrible horrible deaths through the slaughter pipeline. They don't deserve *that*. Over a million horses. A

MILLION, in the last 8 years, it's not even a decade. Don't people understand the horrible things these animals suffer in that fate? Do they just not care?" Sherry began to tear up. She was genuinely passionate about trying to make a difference for horses.

I watched them as they spoke. It was an intense conversation, but also appeared to be one they have had before, maybe regularly. Sherry continued, "And the mustangs! We breed and breed domestic horses and throw those away and then take these mustangs, like Tundra and Aspen's herd and just throw them straight into the pipeline. They have done nothing except benefit public lands! They are PUBLIC lands, but so few stand up to defend these animals. Why? I mean I know not everyone can run a rescue or do big things. But why not speak up? Why not speak on behalf of these animals who are tortured, abused and killed? Look at poor Honey out there. The industry she came from isn't even necessary! Those horses are subjected to sleep deprivation, standing stall confinement, babies thrown away directly to kill pens at such young ages- for PISS. But so many people don't even know what Premarin is. If people would just stand up, make calls, write letters, peaceful protest, *something*. We could band together to END THIS horrendous industry. Why don't people care?"

Joe sighed and looked at his mate. All he could say was "I think the horses ask the same question."

Sherry's journal
I had one of my breakdowns today. Sitting in the quarantine barn, looking at these horses, my heart just melted. It happens from time to time...I break. These horses give us everything, their lives and their deaths, their affection, patience. Everything. I don't understand why

so few people care, so few see. It just breaks my heart and sometimes the reality of the task at hand and the miniscule impact that I make seems so worthless. I love what I do, but I hate that there is even any need for it. These beautiful animals deserve so much better than what humanity gives them. But the horses are such better people than we are. They forgive, they love, they learn and grow and give us chance after chance. I am not as forgiving with my own species as the horses are. I just...wish I could do more.

Chapter 18: Home

Of those that are rescued, there are some that get to go to new homes, begin new lives, there are those who will forever be sanctuary horses, allowed to live out their lives with their horse companions in an environment which is less stressful and healthier for the individual horse. Sometimes rescues make their mark. The horse that was destined for death, becomes a legend. Mot of the time they simply became a legend to their adopter- they become family. Horses are each such amazing individuals and each takes their personal strides and struggles in time.

Rescue horses often get a bad rap as being more of an issue than if you went out to buy a horse from an individual, though often these "rescues" offer the same opportunity as a sale horse. A good portion of horses that go to slaughter every year are rideable, gentle and good minded animals, or young horses that are simply industry excess. Some have papers and obviously good bloodlines. Some don't have papers but obvious good minds. When making decisions on your next equine partner, I hope you look at a "rescue" horse, because the horse you adopt saves not only that horse, but the one that awaits rescue from a kill pen as well. For each horse adopted saves two.

October 25

After vet checks, antibiotics, and more time spent in quarantine, I
have been turned back out with Honey. The excitement from my
friend and my mustang neighbors was palpable. I was glad to be free
from the quarantine stall. I do still have my blanket on, so Honey
investigated it and while she spooked any time I moved for about the
first 3 hours, she eventually settled. There were a lot of questions
about what happened, what they did to me, etc. Everything was
pretty much back to normal by the evening. We all spoke for a long
time, wondering if we were still going to get to go home to our new
lives as adopted horses. Honey was trying to hide her excitement but
you could see it on her face. For the first time in her life, my stoic
friend was looking forward to her future.

236's Journal

*Grandma got turned back out today, she was wearing one of those
weird poofy things that made a scratchy sound. It smelled funny and
every time I touched it it made me jump, but I eventually got use to it.
These people here do weird things to horses. I asked Grandma about it
and she said that it keeps her warm. I was glad for that, I guess I can
get use to it, if it helps her stay warmer. That'll be good for her old
joints and her hurt shoulder. Mostly I was just glad that she was back
with me, I know I have the mustangs, but it wasn't the same. I missed
Grandma.*

October 26

Taylor came early again, as she had the day I had gone into quarantine. She had halters and lead ropes draped over her shoulders. "Okay girls, today is the day." She hung out with us for a few minutes and soon Sherry arrived to our pasture also. Sherry took a halter and lead rope from Taylor and approached me. I didn't bother to run, they had shown me that they will not do any harm. I dropped my head and graciously was led to the gate to wait for my companion.

Honey still takes time and patience to catch. Taylor approached her slowly and stopped about 10 feet from Honey. Honey took a few steps forward which Taylor matched step for step, from her preferred distance. Honey stopped and signaled that she could be approached. Taylor still moved slowly, quietly. She pet Honey on the shoulder, and still Honey tensed. Taylor haltered Honey with a smile and placed her head on Honey's neck. She quietly praised her horse, "that's my girl." Honey looked like she was going to cry for a moment. She is still not use to being someone's favorite horse.

We said goodbye to our mustang neighbors, I smiled at my friend and we were loaded quietly into a waiting trailer. I heard Sherry and Taylor speaking outside of the trailer for a few moments and then it began it's low ruble that told us we were getting on our way. There was a moment of deja-vu when we pulled into the driveway of Denise's house. I looked at the paddock, still half expecting to see Blue, then remembered he was no longer.

Taylor unloaded Honey and put her into Blue's paddock. After a few minutes she came back and unloaded me, I followed happily into my paddock. Denise was waiting at the gate, with apples and a hug. She was still using her mechanical cart that she calls a walker, she looked stronger. Though like me, she had lost a little weight.

I nickered and loved on Denise as Taylor went over and leaned into Honey's paddock feeding her treats and bits of carrot. Honey was looking around and investigating her new home. After about an hour Taylor left, headed back to the rescue. Honey watched Taylor as she went down the driveway and turned onto the road. Denise stayed with me for another 15 minutes or so. She whispered, "I'm glad you're home, it wasn't the same without you." Then she headed into the house.

It was time. I looked at Honey and asked her to follow me to the back of the paddock. She complied and I looked up into the tall tree that stood at the back of our paddocks. When she noticed the halter way up high in the tree, her eyes widened and I told her the story of Hero, just as Blue had told it to me.

As the sun began to set I looked at the tree and back to Honey, when I noticed a slight shimmer in the field a little further out. A breeze had picked up and there was something shiny about 20 yards away. It was a small tree, in it hung a bright blue halter with a small name tag on it. Blue had made it home. As tears silently rolled down my cheeks, I smiled. Sleep well my friend and say hello to Buck for me.

I was home. I now have a home, and a person. I spent the day investigating my new life. It was odd, like I was half way between a dream and awake. Taylor stayed for a little while and returned in the evening to feed us and give me treats. Grandma told me the story about Hero and his tree. An amazing horse, and Grandma has come to be loved by an amazing person.

I hope one day I am strong enough to have a relationship like that with Taylor, but I don't know that I will ever fully get over my fears and anxiety. I do know that she is my person and I will try my hardest to be a good horse. There are so many things I still have to learn, still have to overcome, but I have my family. I have Taylor and I think things will be okay.

November 7

Taylor comes after work every day to spend time with Honey. Honey is making progress with many things, though not with her feet and catching is still touch and go some days. But they are making progress nonetheless. Some days Taylor just comes and sits on the fence. They just quietly enjoy the company of one another. Taylor tells Honey about her day, the other horses that she works with, her hopes for finding them homes. They are good to each other.

Denise is walking without her walker now and today she was able to groom me and spend more time with me during the day. She sung me my song and we walked together around the paddock. She says the doctor won't let her ride yet, but it will come. I am hopeful. I am home.

It has been 5 months since the day that my owner dropped me off at the auction. I am one of the lucky ones, the few who are able to live a new life, escape the nightmare and I couldn't be more grateful. I hope they know that they make a difference. That they save lives. They have given me and Honey the opportunity we could not have dreamed of having without them. I am home, and my friend is healing.

236's Journal

Coming home has been good for Grandma and her person. They have both put weight back on and look happy. They spend a lot of time together. I suppose the change has been good for me as well. Taylor comes and spends time with me, sometimes we work, sometimes she just sits on the fence with her legs across my back. When I get nervous, I look at the Hero tree. It helps me for some reason; to know that horses can overcome, that we can heal and help heal. It reminds me that I will one day maybe have a tree of my own. A place in the ground and in the heart of a person, where I will never be forgotten.

I may have been born just a number, lived as just a number, but I am Honey now and will forever be a name, not a number. It's a dream I never even dared to have, something I can still only whisper lest it be taken and gone forever. I was a PMU factory, but I am becoming a horse.

The winter was a glorious time for learning and love; for Honey and for Lady. They had each other and they had their people. Lady passed quietly two years later, in the spring. After the flowers bloomed, Lady let Denise know that the time was nearing. Denise was able to get on her for one last ride around the paddock and through the field.

Honey continued to struggle with her trust and would take another year before being able to be ridden. She never came around fully and still suffered from nightmares and flashbacks from time to time. Taylor would forever have to be patient in catching, and Honey never fully trusted anyone with her feet, getting bathed or most things that we consider normal routine. Taylor worked patiently and endlessly, but the damage done in Honey's past left too lasting an impression. It was a part of her that she could not escape, a brand on her soul to match the 236 that would forever be present on her hip. She would eternally be wary of all but Taylor.

Grandma was buried in the field, next to Blue, her green halter hung regally and every now and then you could almost see her and Blue running through the field at dusk.

Honey went on to tell the story of Hero, Buck the Mustang and Grandma to 3 horses that were fostered at her home and one special horse that was adopted by Denise 8 years after the passing of Grandma. Now a story that is told along with the others. A legend of humility and honor to help heal the scared and nervous horses who need to hear of the horses who were once Sanctioned For Slaughter.

The Reality

Of the American horses that enter the slaughter pipeline a fraction of those are able to be taken out by rescues and individuals and saved from death. The majority of horses do not get saved, they don't get the family, the happy ever after. They get packed into a trailer and sent to their death, often a horrible and terrifying death.

Overbreeding, industry throwaways, wild heritage and those that are seen as byproducts are cast aside and a blind eye is turned by the public. These horses meet a horrific death for nothing more than our convenience. There is so much that could be done, by a voice, by uniting for the betterment of the horse. We claim that we love these animals, we have used them for everything from plowing fields, colonizing lands, wars, medics, therapy, lessons, show competition partners, everything! We, as a society could stand up on their behalf. I encourage you to do so.

One of our national treasures, the mustang faces not only slaughter, but the vile and horribly traumatizing, sometimes fatal round up methods that are currently being imposed on them. Our government has no respect for the regulations that they themselves have put in place for the protection and maintenance of these beautiful herds. Instead, our mustangs are rounded up by helicopter, horses are maimed and killed by being pushed through barbed wire fencing, pregnant mares are chased forcing them to abort. Horses that are injured or broken, foals that are separated from their mothers- all left behind to die slowly and painfully. Those that are successfully rounded up have now been issued an open ended death sentence by allowing kill buyers to purchase groups of horses for direct shipment to slaughter without even giving these beautiful creatures the dignity of an attempt at a new life of domestication. No they go from wild to vicious death, at the hands of our government and government contractors. Why? Because they know the general public will not speak on behalf of the horse. These things, thanks to advocacy groups and professional photographers are being brought to light. The destruction and genocide of our wild hers are being exposed by the few. Even with the availability of alternate herd management methods, such as darting to regulate reproduction, these archaic practices are what continues. Speak up!

The PMU or Premarin industry is ongoing and while solitary confinement and sleep deprivation are not recognized abuse practices by our government for horses, they are the same methods often used for interrogation which are considered some of the most inhumane. Foals by the thousands enter the slaughter pipeline every year as a byproduct of this industry. This UNNECESSARY industry. With the onset and development of synthetic drugs, plant estrogens and other options available to women to regulate estrogen levels for hormone therapy; this is an industry that continues out of human ignorance and horse abuse. Once the mares are used up, they are also directed to death, no longer a useful part of the industry. To take Premarin, you are medicating yourself with Pregnant Mare Urine, medicating yourself with the lives of horses. This is not just part of the story, this is fact. Please educate yourself on the plight of these horses and help to end this unnecessary abuse and death of thousands of horses each year. Refuse to use.

Nurse mare foals are another notable, though little known victim of the equine industry. Mares are bred every year around the country for the very specific purpose of having their native foal taken from them and replaced with a "more valuable" foal. The foals that are discarded often end up in kill pens, as yet another byproduct of industry, all for the milk of their dam. Milk replacement liquid and pellets are available for orphaned foals, but it's so much easier to throw away a life for the use of the mare.

Since 2010 the United States has shipped over one million horses to out of country slaughter houses. Read that again. Over 1,000,000 horses have lost their lives to this industry which is outsourced and does not require the exported horses to be treated with any kind of humane treatment. They are often abused and tortured before their deaths.

Was that the horse that packed your child all day long through horse camp and begun the passion that your child now has? Was it the horse that taught you to ride? Was it that mustang you never forgot seeing on a trip camping or driving through the desert with your family? Was it the horse that you rooted for in the futurities? Was it a product of unnecessary industries? We export our horses to unknown destinations and death, on average over 100,000 horses every year. Don't they deserve a little dignity? Don't we, as a people, as a nation, have any dignity, or shall we continue to turn a blind eye to the tortures that are whispered in corners but never spoken of in conversation?

So you have this as a result- the death of thousands of foals alone, nurse mare and PMU foals for unnecessary industry. Thousands for the harvesting of urine through abuse. Thousands for the use of the mare. Thousands for the use of the land. Where do you draw the line on a what a horse's life is worth? Where do you stand and decide to make a change? One voice, yours. Change is made though many individuals acting with one goal. Let their life be a goal for you.

While I hope that you have enjoyed the story that this book has created, I more so hope that you have begun to think, to understand the abuses that are so prominent in our country and that you have gained some insight into the struggles of those fighting to make a change, even one horse at a time. Those who rescue, rehabilitate and struggle on behalf of these beautiful creatures are few. I hope you join us in making a difference for their futures.